Screaming Angels

Lazlo Ferran

W & B Publishers
USA

W & B Publishers

For information:
W & B Publishers
9001 Ridge Hill Street
Kernersville, NC 27284

www.a-argusbooks.com

ISBN: 9781635540697

This is a work of *fiction.* All of the characters, organizations and events portrayed in this novel are either products of the author's imagination or used fictitiously.

Book Cover designed by Dubya

Printed in the United States of America

Acknowledgments

Thanks to Derek, Jan and Pedro.

Chapter One

Beside the Bolshiye road Yulia threw down the bicycle and led Yuri into their field.

"Race me to the haystack!" Yuri yelled, his strong legs beginning to pound his feet through the long grass.

"No!"

But Yuri kept running until he grew tired. Following his wake, Yulia reached their patch of long grass and threw herself down, splaying her arms wide and staring up at the endless dome of blue, whose skirt of trees concealed the dome's limit and embraced the two Russian children. A crow wheeled and alighted raggedly on a treetop.

Russia seemed as peaceful as ever, so even with war raging all over Europe, life seemed good on the hottest day of the year, and the good seemed to stretch forever.

Yulia unbuttoned her rough, blue tunic, and ran her finger over the ridges of the embroidered flowers on her white shirt, a Christmas present from her uncle and aunt. She bathed in the sun's heat and throwing her arm over her face to shield her eyes, watched a white butterfly land on a delicate, blue forget-me-not.

Closing her eyes, she watched the red shadows of passing clouds through her lids.

"Come on! I think the field mice have had babies!" Yuri declared, sitting down heavily beside her. "Come on, Yulia!"

"Did you see the white butterfly?" she asked, standing up.

"No."

They both swung to face a sudden blast of sound above the northern hem of trees. Their eyes settled on a sudden, white puff, but then something silver streaked away from the smoke.

"Firework! And a big one!" Yuri shouted above the noise.

"I don't think so," Yulia murmured.

She shielded her eyes from the sun, but still she had trouble following the sleek shape as it shot across their view, higher and higher into the blue dome. But then the jet of flame at its rear went out and it began to tumble.

"Oh!" Yuri said. "I thought it would fly forever! Shall we go and get it?" He made to run after it, but Yulia yelled:

"Stop!"

After a while, two men emerged from the northern hem of trees and strode across the field. Yuri waved to them, but the men either ignored, or didn't see, him. They vanished behind some trees to the south and still hadn't returned after what Yulia guessed to be about half an hour.

"We should go home," she told Yuri.

"Wait. There they are! Let's follow them."

Against her own feeling of caution Yulia followed her younger and more impetuous friend after the men. They emerged from the northern skirt of trees into a smaller field where a grey van waited.

A sturdy man, with a broad face and high forehead below a short crop of dark hair, stood by the van, waiting for the men to bring him the rocket. When it arrived, he checked it over and the two men put the missile in the van. All three men climbed into the cab and the van roared into life. As it skidded past the two children, kicking up the summer dust, the large-broad-faced man waved at them. The van bore the letter RNII on its side.

"Wow! A real rocket!" Yuri declared. He could talk of nothing else on the way home. Yulia could not stop thinking about it either and she would never forget that date; 10 June, 1938, two weeks before her twelfth birthday.

***

Edward Torrens straightened up and grabbed the oily ear of rag that hung out of Don's lab coat, declaring: "It's ready Don, I think. What about you?"

"Aye! Ready, Ed."

Don, the only member of his Rolls Royce Nene team that called his boss Ed, was a working-class Yorkshireman, Edward, a graduate from Dorking. They were Surrey chalk and Yorkshire cheese, but when Don had yelled "Pass Ed!" during a company football match, Edward let the term of endearment go with a smile and they had been close ever since.

"Right! Let's tidy away and get testing!"

The seven men tightened every bolt on the jet engine's outer casing, checked the test stand bolts for tension once more and wiped everything clean. Edward left the test chamber through the partition door and took up station with the rest of the team, behind the control panel. Don checked the last few hose connectors and left the chamber, closing the thick door behind him, but struggled to slide in the heavy draw bolt for a moment, with his back turned. Edward couldn't see what Don was doing.

"Don't touch the master door lock!" Edward joked.

"I never would. There! Got it!"

Edward completed the test form, pushing his spectacles up on the bridge of his nose to focus better:

Monday 22 July, 1946
RB.41 Nene MK.3 throttle-up test.
Attending: Nene team, headed by Donald Hill.
Manager: Edward Torrens.

"Right. Fire her up Don!"

Edward's affable smile belied the tension in the small control room. The cream, concrete partitions had been designed to muffle the sound of WWII piston engines, not stop exotic alloy jet turbine blades, turning three or four times as fast, from exploding. Only a few weeks previously another of Edward's Nene engineers had been injured when a fragment penetrated the wall and ripped part of his cheek away. As Don pressed the starter button, Edward wondered why such an alchemist's brew of wires, alloys and unearthly, screaming power amounted only to the placid sounding 'Nene' in the Rolls Royce executives' minds. Everything went well until Edward yelled into Don's ear at the top of his voice:

"Full power!"

Edward realised he had actually crossed his fingers, just before he heard a high-pitched, metallic 'ping.' He lunged for the red cut-off button and smashed it down with his fist.

Don and the others stared at him with blank expressions, as if trapped in a slow-motion movie clip.

"Duck!" Edward yelled, before dropping to the floor and scrambling under the bench, dragging Don with him.

The turbine's shriek had dropped in pitch about half an octave in those few seconds, but then the air ripped apart with a giant explosion. The sound or rending metal, mixed with the sound of concrete being ripped apart and debris hitting the walls made them shut their eyes and pray.

Eventually, silence returned, followed a moment later by the blaring of alarms and the sound of rushing feet.

"I didn't hear owt!" Don said between coughs. "Bloody good job the engine revs dropped a few thousand! Or else I don't think any of us would be here!"

Covered in white concrete dust and debris, the others scrambled to their feet while Edward looked for his spectacles in the debris. He found the metal frames, but the round lenses were both missing.

"*I* heard it!" he muttered. "A fan blade breaking loose. One of the advantages of managing four test teams and attending *all* tests – not that Sanderson approves. You learn what to listen for! I lost my spectacles and I think some of the glass went in my eye. I can't see!"

"Here, let me help you!" Don replied, putting his arm around Edward.

A First Aid officer quickly arrived and found the single, tiny shard of glass in Edward's eye.

"Hold still Mister Torrens. You're very lucky! It's not penetrated, just lying on the surface!"

"Stupid really! I only need them for close work … I usually take them off for tests."

One of the first people they encountered upon reaching the main shop floor was that of Edward's boss, Sanderson.

"In my office Edward. Five minutes. Get yourself cleaned up. And what's wrong with your eyes?"

Glass went in one. Sore as hell. The other is just weeping in sympathy I think! Ha!"

"Good. Ten minutes then!"

Edward exchanged glances with Don through the eye that was still half open. Don raised his eyebrows.

Ten minutes later, Sanderson didn't waste any time:

"You're a liability Torrens. This isn't the first explosion. Your alloys are too brittle. Nimonic 80a was genius, but these exotics you're trying now are a stretch too far. You're wasting time and money, *my* time and *my* budget! You're a good metallurgist with a bright future, but unless you stop taking such wild risks, I'll have to let you go. Do you understand?"

A defiant glint in Edward's half-open eye must have shown that he didn't, because Sanderson reiterated:

"Yes, *wild*! I know Hooker thinks you'll go far, but I have the final say. This Russian delegation; it's your last chance. I don't know why Hooker volunteered you, but the whole deal is backed by no less than Stafford Cripps!" He added, "*The* President of the Board of Trade and former Minister of Aircraft Production," as if Edward didn't know who the man was. "The whole thing is supposed to cement good relations between our two countries. I don't want *anything* to go wrong. They will *get* their Nene engines and they will have a good time doing so. And *you* will *not* ... balls it up! And remember, they must *not* work out our secret alloys! If they do, we're buggered! We don't mind them having the engines, but we don't want them building their own!"

"Yes sir."

"Don't be late leaving. Be at the main workshop at 4 pm for their guided tour and then go with them to the Midland hotel. Dismissed!"

Edward hated the way Sanderson addressed subordinates as if he were still a Captain on the Army parade ground. When he saw the sour look on Don's face just outside, he knew he couldn't hide the truth from his friend.

"Looks like I'm for the high-jump!" Edward said, dabbing his red eyes with a handkerchief.

"Aye. I heard him. It's not right, shouting like that. And you're the best talent he has! No justice."

By the time he left to join the Russian delegation at 4 pm, Edward's damaged eye had lost its redness and the slight swelling had almost vanished. But his efforts to feel cheerful after Sanderson's attack were failing and the morose darkness, which often rose in him, threatened to overpower his own shadow beside him when he pushed open the double doors and joined the milling visitors in the machine shop.

***

Edward didn't trust women. But only his morose mood led Edward to notice anything unusual about the spectacularly beautiful woman's red shoes that day.

As the Russian delegation filed out of the Rolls Royce factory doors, Artyom Mikoyan paused for a moment, looked up at the sky and declared:

"So is true; always it rains in England!"

Everyone stopped behind the broad Russian while heavy raindrops drummed on the ground. Staring down at the rubber mat and those red, high-heeled shoes, Edward noticed a sliver of something glisten on the wet rubber mat. At first, he assumed it to be a worm and a vivid childhood memory flashed into his mind:

Under the bleaching spotlight of their Dorking patio, his mother, Elizabeth, had paced up and down to show off the shoes that she had just persuaded her husband to buy. She trod on a worm that had been brought up by the evening dew and screamed. Stooping low, she whispered:

"Oh God! I've hurt it, maybe even killed it!"

"Fashion is so cruel!" her husband, Dominic, asserted. His tone, sarcastic, because he did not share his wife's sensitivity to the suffering of beasts, didn't distract Elizabeth from picking up the worm and placing its half-squashed body in the soil, underneath a chrysanthemum.

"I hope you live!" she whispered.

Edward remembered the worm continuing to writhe under the harsh light from the patio for hours, making him adore his mother even more for her tender heart.

That evening Edward imagined his parents' closet to be a witch's cave and crawled in, pointing his torch and Buck Rogers Rocket Pistol ahead. He shone the torch onto the pile of female and male shoes, magical alligators that he had to tame. He carefully lined up the male ones and began doing the same for the females, but he fell asleep before he could complete his quest. His mother found him and scooped him into her arms, declaring:

"Dar-ling! Oh, what a dear! Look Dominic! Come and look!"

She covered Edward's face in sticky lipstick before tucking him up with a bedtime story.

The drumbeat of heavy raindrops drew Edward's attention back to the present. The limousine still hadn't arrived. Mikoyan chatted with Stanley Hooker, a senior Rolls Royce engine designer, but Edward didn't hear what they said. The shuffling of the Russian woman's feet had revealed a second silver sliver. The drums in his head told him this was significant, but he couldn't think why. Then Edward remembered his mother's shoes in the closet that night.

'Her soles were rock hard,' he recalled. 'These might have picked up one metal shaving from a machine and carried it a few yards, but not two, and not this far. These soles look unusually thick.'

With his memory of the last half hour still fresh, he forced himself to go over the woman's movement in the workshop. He remembered Mikoyan, the 'Mi' half of the MiG aircraft company, trying to get close to the lathe and milling machines, before Hooker stopped him. Mikoyan had sent the woman to fetch something for him from the office. When she had returned, Edward thought he recalled her going by mistake to the lathe that cut the turbine blades for the Nene engine. He went over the memory again and recalled more clearly her stopping at that lathe. Hooker had glanced at her and Mikoyan called her away.

'She could have deliberately picked up shavings from the lathe, if her soles were made of soft, thick rubber. Maybe she's a spy!'

The black Daimler arrived and the party climbed in. With difficulty Edward managed to find a seat next to the woman. Finding that her perfume intoxicated him he inhaled deeply while the car glided through the roads of Derby. He couldn't help revelling in the touch on his wrist by her dress, which clung to her like a second skin, but seemed too tight for her to keep still. Edward longed to touch her legs and realised, with surprise, that he felt a deep attraction to her, an attraction that he hadn't felt for any woman in a very long time. The big Daimler engine's power kicked in, making the dress material rustle on her sheer stockings as the woman fell slightly forward. She turned to him, slightly embarrassed, and smiled, but he looked away, out of the window. Her smile reminded him momentarily of his Ewa's.

***

Edward automatically recalled the teary telephone call from his fiancée's mother on 28 March, 1945:

"Another one of them V2 rocket bombs fell in Whitechapel yesterday," her teary voice gasped between sobs. "Ewa was one of those killed. I'm sorry! I have to go!"

He still couldn't order his feelings from that night, when he had felt only sheer disbelief; he thought the War almost over and the V2 attacks finished. Angrily he pushed the memory away.

Since then, Edward had stumbled through a string of failed romances, never quite regaining the optimism of his youth that had helped fire his relationship with Ewa. The string ended in his marriage to a second-generation Czech immigrant, Viktoria. Her lively nature and eagerness to please had bewitched him, but the marriage had quickly turned sour.

Now his confidence had reached an all-time low. Since Viktoria's affair one year before, he had only been granted the privilege of sex with her twice. The previous night had been a, "No!" The price he had paid to keep his marriage intact had become too great.

"It's Rolls Royce for Christ's sake!" Viktoria railed, at breakfast that Monday morning. "One of the richest companies in the world. *Everybody's* heard of Rolls Royce. They *must* be able to pay for your wife to go for one day! It would be wonderful! A luxurious hotel in Derby! A day out from godforsaken Barnoldswick! There's nothing here but a bridge club! I bet the other executives are taking their wives! Besides, I'm proud of what you've achieved. Working with Lucas to come up with magical expansion chambers! No wonder senior management are taking notice." Viktoria's Czech upbringing made her emphasise everything, as if putting up a defence for her life.

"Well I think my promotion has more to do with my acting talented! It *seems* like I'm achieving wonders, because I'm good at taking all the credit for the ideas of *others*! And I told you; there *is* nothing magical about the chambers. That's just what we tell the Russians to put them off the scent of a real secret. It's fake, like almost everything else in my life!"

Edward finished his scrambled eggs on toast and left to catch the milk train to Derby without either of them speaking another word. Only on the train did he guess that Viktoria would have interpreted his last comment to mean that *she* was fake!

'Oh god!' he thought.

***

Edward turned from watching the smoke-stained streets of Derby roll by, to glance at the woman beside him. Her exotic beauty intoxicated him. Like a great, green dragon, he knew it would consume him, if she spoke to him, even once, and thereafter he would be powerless against her, but she remained silent.

'I have to think of myself now,' he told himself. 'This Russian girl's up to something. I know it. Maybe this is my chance, a chance for promotion! And yet if I accused the Russians now, without proof, Sanderson will have all he needs to fire me. No, better to report it to The Vapour.'

Edward read avidly, comics most of all. He often gave secret names to people he didn't like, so at first, he called the man, who had appeared next to him on the Derby pavement, The Creep. But because the man proved creepier than other creeps and had a habit of smoking incessantly, Edward had renamed him. The Vapour told Edward:

"We know about the Russian delegation. I work for the government and we will be watching you and the other Rolls employees, just for protection. You need to be careful; giving information to the Russians is a hanging offence. And if you need help, you only have to call Whitehall 71 and say your name, or drop a crushed matchbox into the gutter."

The last instruction disconcerted Edward most, because it meant they were watching him night and day. He knew they would be watching him now. He tapped the outside of his breast pocket for his spectacle case, a nervous habit.

Outside the Rolls Royce headquarters the limousine stopped and the party disembarked. Trying to make it look like a natural movement, Edward stooped to check the car's carpet where the woman's stilettos had been. He felt somehow disappointed when he saw a few shiny slivers there.

When the party reached the chairman's office, Artyom Mikoyan signed an order that allowed him to leave with ten Nene engines and their spare parts on Saturday and receive fifteen more the following March. Stanley Hooker announced the dinner that would be held in the Midland Hotel that evening and turned to Edward:

"You stay with the delegation Edward. Make sure they're happy. See you at dinner tonight." Hooker's smile reassured the young manager that he was doing alright, so he followed the Russians back to the limousine feeling more confident. But this time the woman sat on the opposite side of the engine designer, Vladimir Klimov, and one other official. Three more Russians sat in front, facing the rear, each wearing a heavy, black raincoat and a short, fur cap. Edward had been briefed that they worked for Russian intelligence, the NKVD, so he tried to avoid making eye contact. Mikoyan sat on the front seat, half turned with his sturdy arm on the seat back, so that he could joke loudly with the other Russian, while the face of the oldest agent, a short, thick-set man with dark hair above a receding hairline, never held anything but a dour expression.

Suddenly the woman seemed to notice something outside the window and cracked a joke in Russian. She laughed, but Mikoyan turned and yelled at her, mortifying the woman into silence and shocking Edward. Mikoyan turned to threaten her for a second time, this time with a glare that looked brutal and terrifying to Edward.

'So she is a victim too,' he thought. 'She's been forced into this, but I can save her. I won't tell The Vapour about my suspicions just yet.'

***

During the lavish roast beef dinner, Edward felt most acutely aware of one thing; his impatience to get closer to the radiant blonde.

She sat next to the dour agent, slightly further down the opposite side of the table from Edward. The Russian had a broad face, deep-set eyes and a mouth that curved downwards at its ends. During the soup, his hand touched Yulia's frequently, but she didn't flinch.

Edward did. Nevertheless, he forced himself to try and get her attention, but she never noticed him until a waiter served coffee. Her glance seemed to speak to him of warmth and curiosity. He felt he had been given the keys to the castle, been given permission to drink down all of her beauty and his heart fluttered in wild abandon.

Whereas her hair had been tied back previously, framing her features, but giving her a slightly serious look, now her mane of wavy, blonde hair rested on her delicate shoulders above a white, ladder-back evening dress, reminding Edward of the variegated gold of ripe corn under an August sun.

'Appropriate perhaps for somebody from the pastoral plains of Russia,' he mused.

Her face would have been considered too thin, were it not for her very large, brown eyes, crinkled at the corner by natural laughter lines. A delicate, concave nose sat above a full mouth, with ruby red lips, whose creases, running diagonally to the fragile side-orbs of her nose, suggested laughter as ready as that of a little girl. Her ears, now concealed by that golden sheaf, had reminded him earlier of fine sea shells, and her neck curved as finely as that of a swan. Edward had to wait for the right moment, and suck in his breath, to dare glance lower.

Below delicate shoulders, narrow but not so much as to make her head look big, swooped a cleavage that out-stripped any man's fantasy Helen of Troy. She laughed at one of Mikoyan's jokes and looked down, before meeting anyone's gaze.

In that moment, Edward had drunk in his most secret fantasy. A night with this woman would answer every question that he had ever asked. He knew he would not dare to look at her again during the meal, so he stared at the starched, white table cloth, twirling his wine glass stem between his fingers for a while, in case any of the party had noticed his forbidden glance. But his exile came not without pleasure. His crotch had stiffened without him noticing, so ardently surged his passion, but its waning proved to be a gradual, down-hill run, full of the recollection of dreams and desires that could last a man a lifetime. At its end, he felt only an indescribable ache, which pressed its wings around his very soul.

Conversation around the table waned, so Edward glanced up, more out of fear than curiosity. Mikoyan raised his hand and everyone fell silent. The large Armenian swept back his flamboyant bang of greased, black hair, turned to Edward and said:

"We are not introduced."

"Edward Torrens."

"You very young. Are you engineer?"

"Yes. I think you could say that."

"And you work on Nene engine?"

Edward nodded, so the Armenian continued:

"Which part you work on?"

This was the moment Edward had nervously anticipated. Noting Hooker's warning expression, he took time to consider before answering:

"The expansion chambers. We have a new technique, part of the reason for the engine's great power output."

Mikoyan studied him coldly and replied:

"Yes! Yes! But we have no problem with expansion chambers! Stator and rotor blades, we have problems with. With such high temperatures as Nene engine, they disintegrate. I understand you have new material ... ?"

"All materials in our engines are top secret, I'm afraid."

Mikoyan played with his glass, looking disappointed. The dour NKVD agent rested his sour face on both his hands and peered into Edward's eyes while the woman leaned back on the chair, so that she could see the side of the agent's head. The NKVD man's look froze the young Englishman's heart and he realised the woman would not glance at him again, perhaps ever.

Mikoyan turned back to Klimov and conversation stuttered into life around the table. But nobody even glanced at Edward.

'What's so fascinating about that fat Russian!' he wondered.

Edward gulped down his dessert of fruit salad and passed on coffee and biscuits, making the excuse that he felt tired. But he didn't go to his Suite. He steeled himself for the task of catching out the Russians. For this he would need the woman's room number and he prayed that she would be staying alone. He stopped at the bar and sipped a double whiskey on the rocks while he waited.

***

Before the limousine had reached the Midland Hotel, Yulia had already become interested in the handsome Englishman. His nose might be considered too big and his eyes too close together, but his short-cropped brown hair and gaunt face gave him a hawkish look, which she liked, and his eyes were blue. She had also noticed the mark on his nose that indicated a man who wore glasses, something else she found attractive. He glanced frequently at her feet, or more accurately, her shoes. At first, she felt glad that he had noticed her feet before anything else.

'Perhaps he will not be like other men, only staring at my cleavage when talking to me. He would have seen my ankles, which I know are fatter than those of most Russian girls, for my height and weight – ugly even.'

"If you have a fault, hide it with a virtue and shout it from the rooftops!" her mother had told her. "My own bust is too small – your daddy told me so – so I wear a padded brazier, which makes me look like Jane Russell!" With this, Yulia's mother cupped her bust and jiggled it up and down with a glint of joy in her eyes. "It makes all the locals jealous and your daddy proud."

Hence the red shoes. But the discomfort of walking on shoes with metal shavings embedded in the soles had stung her feet and stilted her gait, making her feel even more nervous. Her NKVD training had shown her how to observe without being noticed, so she had seen the young man stoop to check the floor of the car before climbing out at the Rolls Royce headquarters. Now she had the hardening conviction that he had noticed something, and not her ugly feet.

'He must have seen the shavings!' she realised, horrified. 'What if he works out what I have done?'

But Yulia knew she was beautiful. This fact had always been her ace in any game with men. When she walked into a room she knew every man would watch her, respect her for her power. Her beauty had, however, proved to be a glass cage in the game of life; she looked at everything through the filter of men's desire. She could always tell when men were staring at her, even when her eyes were closed. Only very rarely did a man *not* stare at her, and then only because he tried too hard to ignore her. But this young man *had* ignored her until he saw her feet. Perhaps, she speculated, because he felt sad about something, he had been staring at the ground and noticed her shoes, the one eventuality she hadn't anticipated.

Yulia resisted the urge to chuckle at the coincidence in the car, but consequently half-choked. The young man glanced at her with concern on his face, so she had to smile. He didn't smile back. This made her feel anger, the same anger she felt when her uncle Makar told her she was fat. How clever he had been.

***

When Yulia heard from her uncle in the NKVD that he was involved in planning a mission to England, and to Rolls Royce in Derby no less, she couldn't wait to get involved. She begged him to talk to the right people, move mountains, and he had.

Her childhood in Porozhek had been dreary at best, and at worst, a nightmare. Her other uncle, Makar, ran the grocer's shop in the nearest big town, Tosno, and came to visit a few months after she had seen the rocket. Scared of his unfamiliar face, she went to hide in the shed with their old goat.

"Hello Yulia. Do you still have the football?" he said, when he found her.

"No. I gave it to the boys to play with and they punctured it."

"Oh. I see. Are you going to milk that old goat? What's her name?"

"Her name is Udashka!"

They both laughed.

"Does she always kick then?"

"Only strangers."

The joke had taken away Yulia's fear of her strange uncle. She looked more closely behind the bushy black beard, which had been greased back in typical Russian macho style, and could see the glint of intelligent curiosity in his eyes. His ham-sized hands pressed against two oak pillars of the shed, making her imagine that he could bring the building down like Samson, if he wanted. The thought excited her strangely.

"You are becoming pretty!" her uncle declared.

"Oh. Do you think so?"

"Except your ankles look a little fat. But I can't tell about your legs under that stupid regulation tunic!"

"Oh." Yulia felt a little disappointed and wanted to look at her own ankles to see if she agreed with her uncle, but felt too embarrassed, so continued to play the frayed strands of a coiled rope between her fingers. She felt hot in the shed, but the bead of sweat on her forehead still surprised her.

"So are you going to milk her?" her uncle continued, crouching by the tethered goat.

"I don't usually. But it doesn't look as if mother has done it, so I *could*. Wait!"

Yulia cast around for the wooden pale and found it. She lifted the pale, placed it between Udashka's hind legs and dragged the milking stool over to sit on. Her uncle's jumper sleeves were rolled up and she could see his enormous biceps bunch and flex as he kept his balance on his heels by gripping his knees. She wondered what his biceps would feel like to touch, but would only have asked, if he had been younger.

Makar crabbed over to crouch beside her as she began squeezing the goat's udders. After a few squeezes, the first of the creamy milk spattered the pale bottom and spread out to form a shallow pool. He suddenly reached out and pulled her tunic up over her knees, such a sudden movement that she didn't consider stopping him. They both studied her thigh while she continued to milk.

"Um. Maybe not so fat, but still a little," Makar remarked.

"Oh. Sorry."

Yulia quickly brushed down the hem of her tunic. She thought this might have looked to her uncle as if she wanted to hide her shamefully fat thigh, but she felt embarrassed by his stare. However, to her dismay, when she glanced at him again, she saw him brazenly staring at her chest, whereupon she stood up quickly, so that he couldn't touch her there. Makar became very angry and left, slamming the barn door behind him and racing the engine of his van as he drove away. Her father avoided her for almost a week. She was thirteen.

***

The fetid odour in the shed that day still stuck to Yulia's memories like ordure. But yes, she knew she would be able to make the young man keep quiet, as long as he sought her out, and Kirill had already found out that the young man would be staying in the Midland Hotel until Saturday. He would come to her before then.

The limousine stopped outside the Hotel and Yulia followed the NKVD General to his Suite, where she asked him to find out the young man's name and more about his background.

"You think he knows something?" the General asked her.

"I am not sure comrade Bregovsky. It's best for us to be prepared. Tell Gregori to be prepared for Plan B."

Kirill Bregovsky levelled his gaze at her and she met it boldly. After a few moments, he broke away to get dressed for dinner, her signal to leave.

The dinner bored Yulia. Once she had decided when and how to smile at the young man, she had nothing left to do, but tolerate Kirill's touches and smile at the Rolls executives when appropriate. Her smile for Edward went well, although she couldn't be quite sure that the instant of pure innocence she gave him was false, as it usually was.

Yulia's only awkward moment came when the young man refused to help Mikoyan with information about the turbines. After this the Russian designer pulled away from her, forcing *her* to try and touch *his* hands, something she hadn't done before. The mock-paternal approach to their relationship that he seemed to prefer required her to feign a certain chaste intimacy with him, but she could tell he felt angry when he rebuffed any further touches. She hoped she had mollified him somewhat and withdrew into herself.

At first, her thoughts circled around the young Englishman, whom she now knew to be called Edward. His dark hair lacked the flamboyant bang or 'wave' that wealthy Russian men always sported, something about him that pleased her, but she could see insecurity and deception in his blue eyes, although she felt the deception must be for the other members of the party. She considered herself to be a good judge of men and beneath all the complex layers of emotion reflected in his eyes, she believed she had seen the steady light of honesty.

Yulia still wanted to believe good men existed, but she found it hard to do so. She let her mind wander back to her home village of Porozhek. She missed the endless sweep of green forest and the pretty, wooden chalets. She had met many senior NKVD officers who might have appreciated one as a dacha, but she intended keeping Porozhek a secret until she had earned enough roubles to buy one herself.

Her memory cast back yet further, to the night after seeing the rocket. At first, she couldn't sleep, but must have drifted off eventually, because she had a dream that seemed real, in which she flew on a witch's broomstick. Flight seemed effortless, so she soared higher and faster, across all of Russia and then Europe. Whichever way she wanted to go, the broomstick would take her. Everything she saw seemed a darker or lighter shade of black, but also somehow magically beautiful. She felt a cool power and energy course through her, so she flew higher and higher, until Yuri's voice warned her that she had flown too high. She laughed at his uncharacteristic caution, but then she jolted awake in her bunk.

"You were dreaming Yulia!" her little brother, Demitri, whispered. "I was scared for you."

She lay awake, wondering about the strange dream. It had been so vivid that she wondered if she were sleeping now.

She snapped back to the Midland Hotel dinner and glanced at Kirill, thinking that he reminded her of Sergei Korolev, the rocket designer, who she had later learned waved at them from the van on the day of the rocket launch.

But the memory of her uncle visiting again in the autumn of that year chased that happy memory from her mind. This time he had brought his own goat and led it out of the grocery van on a leather leash. Yulia laughed at the irony, but her laughter turned to anxiety when she heard them arguing in the parlour. She put her ear to the door and heard Makar's raised voice say:

"Shut up you foolish woman. This is no concern of yours. Do you want the goat or the money?"

The first icy blasts of the winter had begun, so it would have been dangerous for Yulia to stand outside for long, wearing just her tunic. She pushed the door open and coughed loudly.

All three combatants stopped to stare at her. Her mother's weatherworn face cracked into a smile, but her uncle whispered something into her father's ear and together they left the room.

"Go to your room and stay there," her mother whispered, with a note of warning in her voice.

Yulia did as her mother told her, but then her Uncle came and …

She had to thrust the thought of what he did to her down to the very bottom of her soul, and jerked in her seat with the effort. Kirill snapped his face around to stare at her, so she grinned artlessly, as if she had just been falling asleep.

She wanted to be held, but had to settle for stroking the cool surface of a silver spoon.

***

Edward followed the Russians when they left the restaurant and saw the woman enter Suite 36 with the dour NKVD agent. Edward's Suite, 31, was on the same floor. He sat on the edge of his bed, wondering what to do. He hadn't even unpacked his suitcase.

'I have to confront her,' he thought. 'I have to talk to her and give her a chance to confess. I'm the only one who can ... .'

He strode to the door before completing the sentence, walked the short distance to her Suite and pressed his ear to the white-painted panel, but could hear nothing from within. His heart seemed to be trying to pound its way out of his chest, but shaking his head at his own indecision, he tapped his knuckles on the door.

"Da?"

"Hello. It's Edward Torrens ... . From Rolls Royce. I'm so sorry to disturb you ... ."

He expected an angry NKVD agent to wrench the door open and glare at him, but the sweet face of the Russian woman confronted him:

"Oh, hello. Come in!"

"Thank you. Am I ... disturbing anything?" he said, casting a long sweeping glance around the reception room for Russian men.

"No. But you caught me unprepared," Yulia lied. "Wait a moment!"

Wearing only a white bath robe and with her blonde tresses piled on top of her head, she cleared a space amid copies of Vogue and Bazaar on the sofa.

"Sit down please," she said in impeccable English.

"I would rather stand ... ."

"Alright. Do you want a drink?"

"No thank you. I have come to ask you something."

Edward tried to feel comfortable, but found his weight balanced well neither on one foot nor the other. He suddenly felt like a Roman gladiator in a vast arena.

"There's something I want to ask you … ," he began. "No tell you … . I'm *sure* I will be listened to, if I'm correct."

Yulia passed him, seeming not to hear, so Edward touched her arm to stop her. She smiled thinly and obediently perched on the edge of a lavishly upholstered lounge chair.

"Sorry. You have my complete attention," she replied, lifting her gaze to stare directly into his eyes. "I like men who wear glasses. They are thinkers! I prefer men who can think to those with big muscles and no brains! And you have such lovely blue eyes!"

Edward blurted:

"I saw you, on the mat at the entrance to Rolls. Two slivers of metal by your shoes. This is *not normal*! There were two or three more on the carpet in the car! Do I make myself clear?"

Edward turned around to see her clasping her knees with her hands. She didn't reply. He looked around, as if expecting Russians to burst through the door.

"Perhaps I should go," he said.

"No, wait!" she replied, jumping up. "Let me fix you a drink!" Her robe parted slightly, revealing more of her cleavage. "The Hotel gave us a complimentary bottle of vodka, which isn't too bad."

"Thanks, Miss … ?"

"Call me Yulia. My last name is Panedolia, if you want to know it."

"It sounds Greek, but pretty. Yulia sounds pretty."

"I was warned about charming Englishmen."

"Ha!" Edward took the glass from her hand and tasted the clear spirit, before grimacing. "Do you have lemon juice or water?"

"I don't have lemon. Can I use English tap water? I mean; is it safe here?"

"I think so. We're certainly told so."

"Oh. Alright then. Wait."

Yulia took his glass and topped up the vodka with water from the bathroom sink tap.

Edward took a sip and rolled the cold liquid around on his tongue. He heard a train whistle and thought he heard the slow, deep 'chuff, chuff' of a train moving. Yulia heard something different and went to the door. Confused, Edward wondered if he *could* have heard a steam engine's exhaust blast. Ignoring Yulia, he looked to one of the sash windows and for the first time, noticed that it was open.

"Da!" he heard Yulia say, with the door held open a crack. She followed this with a torrent of Russian, to which a deep voice that Edward recognised as Mikoyan's, occasionally replied, before she closed the door. "Is it good?" she said, returning to her chair.

"Sorry, I didn't notice." Edward sipped again. "Yes, I can confirm that it *is* good. Unusual … . I don't think I have had vodka before. What's it made from?"

"Potato skins, usually."

"Oh, I see."

"You were saying?"

"Um. Yes. As I was saying … . Um … ."

"Shall I tell you how I came to work for Kirill?" Yulia interjected.

"Kirill?"

"General Kirill Bregovky. I am not so naïve as to think that you don't know he is an NKVD agent."

Edward's hesitant nod was all she needed. "It all started when I saw my first rocket launch, in 1938. I

come from a little village, not far from Leningrad … .
You know where that is?"

"I'm not sure."

"Northern Russia, but not far from Poland and
Moscow. My village is very small and nothing ever
happens there. Well, not much anyway … . One day my
friend Yuri – he was, is, two years younger than me –
and I went for a ride on my father's old bicycle. There is
a field where we liked to roll and play. All little children
do this, even English children, yes?"

"In summer, yes."

"Da! I mean; good! England is not so boring
then! Ha! We were running, actually, no, Yuri had just
been running, but now we were walking when we saw a
silver – it was no more than a flash of silver in the sky.
It was hard for us to follow with our eyes, but Yuri
became very excited. He jumped up and down and ran
after it. But do you know what I felt?"

"No."

"I wanted to know how the rocket worked and
whether it could reach the stars! Ha! I am such a
dreamer! Anyway, we saw two men and followed them
to a truck. A man waved at us. On the side of the van, it
said 'RNII.' Later, when I went to Leningrad, I found
that this meant the 'Jet Propulsion Research Institute.'
Sergei Korolev was the name of its head and I found a
photograph of him. He is the one who waved at me. He
became my hero from that day! The Institute had
government backing, so I knew that getting into the
Army might allow me to meet Korolev. When
Leningrad agents came to our village searching for
engineering students two years later, Yuri signed up!
Much later I wrote to him and he sent for me. It was
Yuri who helped me to join the Army." Yulia frowned.
"Korolev was the first to achieve a launch of a liquid-

fuelled rocket. I always wanted to be an engineer, since I was a little girl. Then I wanted to be a rocket designer."

Edward had been surprised by Yulia's use of the phrase 'liquid-fuelled,' but put it down to her absorption of Soviet propaganda, shrugged and replied:

"Oh. I'm not keen on rockets … ."

Edward left the comment to hang, which only intrigued Yulia more, but she decided to tuck the detail away for later.

"It doesn't matter," she continued. "Russia is very different to Great Britain! Tell me about *your* childhood."

Edward wasn't keen to be deflected from his interrogation, even less to talk about his childhood, but they both sensed the presence of a determined adversary and both were as keen as the other to explore the other's strengths and weaknesses, so he nodded. He knew himself to be an introvert, but he could think of several events during his childhood that made him look like an indestructible extrovert and given him a confidence that had made him into a good leader. He decided to serve one of these up to her on a plate.

***

Edward's memory of the event remained particularly vivid.

"I don't know why, but you made me think of something that happened with my brother – my younger brother, Sam," he began.

"Go on … ."

"We used to stay in the country, when I was about eleven. There was a river, with an island. I always wanted to explore it, but we didn't have a boat and dad said it was too dangerous to swim in the river, because it was fast-flowing. Anyway, there was a tall tree, an elm,

I think, on our bank and its branches reached right over the river to touch the branches of another tree – I can't remember what type of tree – on the island. Sam and I used to climb this elm tree, because it was so old that some of its branches hung down, almost to the ground. I was the best climber in school. Sorry, I'm boasting, but everyone said I was. Maybe I got overconfident, because this day – it was a hot one; I know that because I only had my t-shirt on – I didn't just want to climb to the top, but I climbed out on one of the thicker branches, about two-thirds of the way up. 'What are you doing?' Sam yelled. I didn't reply, because I didn't know what I *was* doing. I seemed to be in some kind of dream and felt I couldn't stop and shouldn't. I don't know, it was strange … . Sam kept shouting that I should stop and come down, but I kept on going. Soon I was on the thinnest branches, which were dipping and waving around. I don't know how I stayed on! They should have snapped, but they didn't. It was like a dream. And I held my breath and then I was on the branches of the other tree and before I knew it, I had climbed down onto the island."

"Wow! How did you feel?"

"Well, at first, I didn't feel that different. But then I knew my heart had been pounding like crazy and I hadn't even noticed. Sam was staring at me like I was a ghost and then I looked up at the branches and I couldn't see how I did it! I could never have done it again. Something happened to me that day. Sam still talks about it."

"How did you get back?"

"Well that's the funny thing. On the opposite side of the island was an old bridge, which led to a path. I followed this and came to the main road. It took me an hour to find the way back to our lodge. Sam and I didn't tell my parents, so they never knew. My dad would have killed me!"

"He was strict?"

"Well, my mother was an Angel, but my dad was – well, how do I describe him? He is full of himself and full of fantasies. He made some money as a beer salesman – even went to America just before the War – so we had a nice house in Dorking ... . Put it this way, when he was drunk he liked to be called Major Torrens. You know why?"

"No ..."

"He served in World War One, but only achieved the rank of Corporal. But after the War, he signed up for the Volunteer Reserve. They met every so often and he eventually got promoted to Captain. But it wasn't a real rank; I think they just gave it to him for longevity. Anyway, just before the last war, they said they would promote him to Major, if he volunteered for full-time service, but he never did. So now he tells everyone he's a Major. That's what he's like. He stretches every truth until it becomes a lie ... in my opinion."

"But he is good at selling."

"Yes."

"And your mother loves him."

"Yes. She did. But she loved all creatures great and small! Ha!"

"Was she very nice?"

"She was adorable. She never shouted or lost her temper with me – I heard her shout at dad a few times ... ."

"And your brother?"

"I have a sister too, Susan. She is the youngest and she's *so cute*. She really makes me laugh, but I don't see enough of her. Sam? He's always been my best *mate*. There was another ... incident ... like the tree one that tells you what Sam's like. He hasn't a hint of ego.

He never thinks much about himself. He's happiest helping others, including Susan. He *really* takes care of *her*! Anyway, he had really put on weight by the time of this second adventure. Again, it involved a river, on a waste ground near a factory in Dorking. We were bored, so I suggested we build a raft. We made it from pallets and old oil-drums, which we bound together with twine ... ."

"Twine?"

"String."

"Alright. Go on."

"So we put this thing in the water – it was only a stream about twenty feet wide – and the thing floated nicely. I went first and I had a paddle made from a plank of wood. I must say; the raft sank underwater at one corner and it was tricky to steer, but I reached the other side without getting wet and Sam pulled it back with a rope that he tossed over. Remember, he was fatter and heavier than me at this time. He climbed on and ... well ... he started to sink straight away! But he wasn't angry. He just laughed and went completely in! We just laughed all the way home. He was so funny. Mum laughed too, but dad wasn't so amused ... . I don't know why, but I find you very easy to talk to. I should really be asking you about something else. But I don't want to."

"Oh. Maybe we will talk about that soon. Tell me a bit more. *Please*?"

"You know, I'm not sure you're not trying to side-track me!"

Yulia furrowed her eyebrows and stared at the ceiling. "I was warned about double-negatives. English speech can be so *indirect*. *Too* polite to understand. Let me think about *that*. And what is 'side-track?'"

"Sorry. To divert."

"Alright. Hm. Well, I wasn't trying to do that. I just like listening. We never get to meet people from England normally. Russia is beautiful and I love it, but it has deficiencies."

"Hm. Well, what would you like to know?"

"Holidays! Tell me about one. We never have them. Only the rich have them."

"I'm sure you're just teasing me! Oh, well. Let me think. Sidmouth, 1933! Sidmouth is a holiday town, on the coast. The beach doesn't have sand, but pebbles. That's not very comfortable, but at least the sand doesn't get into your sandwiches! We had been going there almost every year since I was three. Dad liked it, because one of the Royal Family stayed there, so it was quite up-market. Enough for his tastes anyway. The weather had been changeable just before we went; I remember my parents arguing in the kitchen whether we should go. Mum didn't want to go because she thought it would rain. Anyway, it was the summer holidays and I was bored of playing at home, so I wanted to go. Do you have summer holidays?"

"At school? Yes, it varies, but in a farming community like ours, it is more than two months. The children are needed for the harvest."

"Oh, of course! Well, it's hard for me to describe how idyllic Sidmouth could be. I'm no poet! We stayed in a lovely old hotel, set back from the sea-front, called Green Gables. It looked like an old Empire pavilion and had sweeping lawns and a grass bank, down which Sam, Susan and I would frequently roll, making our clothes green! I don't know what date we arrived that particular year, but I remember thunderstorms on the first night and then it got really hot. The days just seemed to roll on forever; playing in the foaming waves on the beach, idly window-shopping, walking on the cliff-tops, fishing and just lying on the grass at the hotel, reading a book!

Oh, and they used to play gramophone records at breakfast and evening meals; Beethoven's Pastoral Symphony, last movement." Edward hummed the tune. "Da-da, de da-da, de da, de da, de da … . Do you know it?"

"Ha! Ha! Yes, it is famous in Russia too. But what is 'window-shopping?' Shopping for windows?"

"Ha! Ha! No, looking at things in shops without actually buying anything. Do you do that?"

"In Porozhek? That's my village. No! We don't have any shops! The nearest are in Tosno, but they often don't have windows and the storekeepers don't like you doing that. Anyway, who wants to look at vegetables, or tins of food?"

"You don't have dress shops?"

"There may be, but my family is poor. I have shopped in Moscva – Moscow. As you saw at dinner, Mikoyan buys me *nice* dresses!"

"Oh, yes."

"Well, your childhood sounds idyllic, like a dream. Just as you said! Where are Sam and Susan now?"

"Well, Sam has joined the RAF – he's studying at Cranwell. Susan is training to be a nurse."

"And were there any girls in … Sidmouth?"

"You *are* clever. I was going to tell you about her, but I thought not to."

"Don't be shy. Why should you leave out somebody who made you happy?"

Edward blushed deep red and coughed once before answering:

"Could I have just one more vodka please?"

"Of course."

This interlude gave him more time to measure out how much he would reveal in his story. He knew that the time had come to steer the subject back to the reason for his visit, so he worked out how to link back. Yulia put as little water in the vodka as she thought she could get away with.

"So?" she said, handing him his drink and tucking her legs under herself on the chair.

"Well, it was one of those days. You know? I was lying on the lawn, looking up at the sky and, well, just drifting. I don't remember any distinct thoughts. The sun just does that to you, sings you into a dream."

"Ha! You have a lovely way of using words. You should be a writer!"

"Oh no. I would be hopeless! I don't have the patience and I'm not very poetic!"

"Hm."

"Anyway, I thought I saw movement and rolled over to look. This girl – she looked like Susan – wearing a white summer frock, came toward me. But it wasn't Susan. And this girl had a halo of gold hair, like yours, but the sun shone straight through it when she stood over me. I don't remember what she said, but we became friends. Her name was Amanda, or Sandy, or something simple like that."

"Friends? Did you kiss her?"

"Well, yes. I think I did. My first kiss. I don't remember much; sitting on the bed, talking about school and boys, the sun streaming in and both of us being relaxed … . I think I touched her hand and she smiled at me, so I kissed her, without thinking. But listen, great as these memories are, it's not what I came to talk to you about. It's getting late and I need an answer!"

Chapter Two

"What answer do you need?" Yulia asked.

"Listen; I'm very loyal to Rolls Royce and I have not just me to think about, but my family. This could go very badly for us if I just … *let this go!*"

Edward paced up and down in front of Yulia, but she only smiled. Her smile reminded him of someone's. She ventured:

"Listen, there is no point in getting angry. I am sure we can come to an agreement. Is your sister beautiful?"

"What?"

Yulia's conciliatory tone, combined with the incongruous question, forced Edward to sit down. Now he felt caught between the hope of a solution and a veiled threat.

"I mean; is she more beautiful than me?"

"I don't think that's relevant!"

"Just be patient. Is she?"

"Well, she's pretty, but not so pretty as you!"

"You think I am pretty?"

Edward swirled the last of his vodka around the bottom of the glass and fixed his gaze on the patterns it made.

"Let me fix you one more," Yulia offered.

Edward felt tempted to tell her about Viktoria, but remained silent. Yulia emptied the bottle of vodka on the shelf and handed him a glass of almost neat spirit.

"Let me turn the light down. It's been a long day!" she whispered.

She stood and walked to a sideboard where she switched on a table lamp. Her bathrobe had become so loose that Edward could see almost to the top of her alabaster thigh when she passed him. She walked to the door and switched off the main light, leaving the room bathed in warm mid-tones of brown, reflections from the furniture and wallpaper.

Sitting on the arm of the chair, she crossed her legs and balanced her arms on her knees, clasping her hands together. He had expected her to lounge languorously on the chair in order to seduce him, but instead she seemed to focus all her attention on Edward.

"So, am I pretty?" she asked again.

Edward tried to stare at his drink and replied:

"Eh hm! If I were to find out one of the delegation has been trying to steal information about the alloy we use in the form of metal shavings ... . With these shavings, your engineers could reverse engineer our rotors and build an engine, even a *better engine* for themselves. I would *have* to report it!"

"Of course! I would expect that! Is my English good? I am very attracted to Englishmen. When do you leave the Hotel?"

"Saturday."

"We can spend some time together before then?"

Edward's fingers involuntarily relaxed around his drink, so that he had to catch the falling glass with his other hand, spilling some of clear spirit in his effort. He licked his finger-tips and told her:

"I'm married. Her name's Viktoria."

"Oh. But ... ." Yulia pointed to his hand.

"No wedding ring? No. I stopped wearing it. Bravado really."

"Sorry? I don't understand."

"It's nothing. Listen, I can't answer your questions. I'm interested in only one. You keep offering me just enough to make me stay, but not enough to make me go away! Which do you want?"

"I don't want you to go *away* ... ."

"Okay, maybe I worded that badly. I mean I'm getting tired of being *teased*. I will have to report you, if you don't reassure me you know *nothing* about what I have told you! And I'm beginning to think you *do*!"

Yulia did her best to look as if she were about to cry. She replied, using a voice full of cracked emotion:

"If I helped you, could we spend some time together?"

"Well ... *if* I can see the red shoes first."

"It's a deal!"

Yulia stepped into the bedroom and returned with the pair of red shoes. She placed them into Edward's nervous hands and sat down, facing him, while he looked them over.

"Seems like the same pair," he observed. "But maybe you had two?"

Edward held the shoes tentatively, as if they were somewhere between a pair of nuclear bombs and fine Rembrandts. He could smell a faint odour of salty sweat, mixed with a delicate floral fragrance, new leather and something else, which he couldn't place. Edward turned the red shoes over and stared at the soles, but he could only see faint indents where metal shavings might have been embedded. Shaking his head slowly, he declared:

"These soles look very thick ... ."

"Oh."

"Why is that?"

"I don't know. These are the latest fashion in Leningrad."

She snatched away the shoes.

Edward replied, "I think I have to tell my superiors," and stood up.

"Okay. But I know *nothing* about any theft from the factory Edward. I *swear* it! And Bregovsky, I mean *Kirill*, gave these shoes to me. He asked me to wear them. I should have been suspicious! They are hardly the ideal shoes for walking around an engineering workshop!"

"Good bye Miss Pana … ."

"Pan-*e*-dolia. Good bye Edward. It's been lovely meeting you."

After Edward had gone, Yulia stared into space, mulling over her own thoughts for a few precious moments while waiting for the inevitable. It came when Kirill burst into the room and shouted:

"What did he say? Does he know anything? He was here for a *long* time!"

"He doesn't *know*. He just suspects," she snapped back.

"What about?"

"The shoes. I showed him."

"*What*? You crazy bitch!"

"There was nothing there. Where are the filings now?"

"You don't need to know *that*! Hm. Artyom and his men are analysing them. But they're useless without the engines! We must keep them off the trail until Saturday."

"Find out more about him; more about his family and friends. Something I can use."

"Alright. But where has he gone now?"

"I don't know. He was unhappy, but I think he won't do anything tonight."

"Damn! You stupid bitch! I will get Gregori to watch his rooms. Wait here!"

"I'm not going anywhere!" Yulia whispered after the disappearing Russian. Moments later he returned to continue questioning her:

"What did you tell him?"

"Nothing! Of course! Give me time comrade. I know this type of man. I can control him. He *won't* talk."

"I hope you are right Yulia. Things will go badly for you, and *me*, if he does! Don't forget *why* you are here. I am thinking you are already fond of this young *Englishman*, and *England*!"

Yulia wanted to tell Kirill that he was too suspicious, but he would never have taken criticism from her. Whereas he called her Yulia, she could only call him comrade, privately and in public.

'Like most Russian men," she reflected. "And it's not just paranoia!'

Kirill saw the empty vodka bottle and held it up, glaring at Yulia.

"Drunk too!" he accused. "Let me smell your breath."

He surged toward her and she thought he would hit her, but at that moment they both heard soft raps on the door.

"Come!" Kirill replied, stepping back and straightening his tie.

One of the two lower-ranked NKVD agents entered the room, nodding deferentially. Stocky and short, his face looked bland and would have seen vaguely familiar to anybody. He glanced at Yulia, but she looked away.

"Yes Gregori?" Kirill asked.

"Torrens has left his rooms and gone to the bar."

"Alright Yulia. Get dressed! You're going down there and I don't want you coming back without being sure, or without *him*; one of the two! We *have to* succeed. Comrade Stalin is counting on us. Who would ever have thought a low-ranking engineer would be the one to catch our scent. It's a disaster!"

Gregori's jaw muscles knotted and unknotted.

***

Alone in his Suite, Edward imagined Bregovsky killing Yulia, if she told him anything, or if the Russian even suspected anything. For this reason, he decided he couldn't tell The Vapour yet.

"This is stupid! Now I'm worrying about her! But maybe she likes me? Maybe she could even love me? I *could* probably love her, but I have a wife. Oh! These ideas are not worthy of a mature adult."

He sat on the edge his bed for a moment, but jumped up, saying to himself:

"I can't sleep right now. I need to think. And this room's depressing."

He went downstairs, intending to go out for a walk, but the bar was still open, even though midnight had passed. The barman quietly wiped washed glasses clean while Edward sipped a glass of gin and tonic.

Staring deep into his glass of spirit, he looked up with astonishment when the kaleidoscope of barroom images in the cut glass became a distorted version of Yulia's pretty face.

"May I join you?" her soft soprano voice asked. "Kirill said he will come down in a minute. I .... I couldn't sleep."

Edward wondered if this could be a lie:

'Why would she come down for what ... ?' He glanced at the clock behind the bar; thirty-one minutes after midnight. 'Can only be one drink at the most?' He nodded, before lifting his face to smile at her.

"Am I too late to order drinks?" she asked the barman. A smooth smile slipped away from the corners of his mouth underneath a brown moustache, which added to Edward's impression that the man came from somewhere near the Mediterranean.

"For you pretty lady, I think a glass of white wine would not upset the management too much!"

"Make it two; my boss will be down in a few minutes."

The barman turned to pour the drinks.

"You see?" she said, turning to Edward. "My skills in Moscow bars work here too! Ha! Ha!" She paused. "You don't know what to say! It's like a little cave in here, isn't it?"

"I suppose so."

"Have you been thinking about me?"

"Actually, yes."

"Good!" Yulia sipped from her glass of wine and grimaced. "Oo! Sweet!"

The light from a chandelier cut out for a moment and a heavy figure slouched over the bar stool next to Yulia, bellowing:

"Bar tender! Gimme a whiskey!"

"Sorry sir. The bar's closed."

Edward twisted his head and leaned back to get a better look at the intruder:

'Oh no!' he thought. 'A drunk executive! That's all we need!'

"Hello ... *lady*! You're the Russian bit, aren't you?"

"I am sorry. I don't understand what 'bit' means," Yulia replied.

Edward nervously played with his glass.

"I mean; you're part of the deal, aren't you?"

"You must be mistaken. I am the secretary of one of the officials in the party and he is coming down in a few minutes, so you should behave yourself and act like the English gentlemen we hear so much about!"

The barman shot a sly smile at Yulia. Edward leaned close to her ear and whispered:

"Well played!"

But the Rolls Royce executive wasn't going to be deterred so easily. He swung to face her and engaged her in meaningless conversation about her visit to London, but when, after five minutes, Bregovsky hadn't arrived, he grabbed the second glass of wine.

"I presume this is his, but he isn't coming, is he? Mind if I have it?"

Yulia relented with a sigh and turned away from the intruder, but the heavy man grabbed her shoulder and swung her back to face him.

Edward knew the man far outranked him, but his missing tie and jacket, unbuttoned shirt and stench of whiskey seemed to even the odds. He stood up and told the executive firmly:

"Leave her alone!"

"Oh yeah? Who says? She your woman?" the man leered.

"It's okay," Yulia interjected. "It was I who was rude." While she spoke to the drunk, she sought Edward's hand with the one that she concealed behind her back. Their fingers touched only briefly, but it was the touch of allies. Edward sat down and sipped his drink while Yulia patiently fielded the man's advances.

It wasn't long before the executive announced he was visiting the, "Little Boy's Room!"

"Let's go! Quick!" Yulia announced, giggling and grabbing Edward's arm. Before he could stand, she had vanished down the corridor, so he ran after her, laughing.

"You handled him like a pro, you cheeky, little nymph!" he blurted, when he caught her.

"What is a nymph?" she said, staring into his eyes.

"Doesn't matter."

They crept quietly to the stairs while the barman made the most of the opportunity, whisking away the half-empty glasses and rolling down the bar's shutters.

"We made it!" Edward joked as they tumbled onto her sofa.

"Do you want another drink?" Yulia asked. "Oh wait! I don't have any! Ha! Ha!"

Edward laughed too. "I don't want any more; I've had enough anyway."

"Let me just change into something ... else!"

They both laughed at this too.

"I'm so tired!" she said, disappearing into the bedroom.

Minutes later she emerged wearing loose-fitting, cloth trousers and a primrose blouse that had seen better days.

"Wow! Women never wear stuff like that here, unless they work in the garden!" Edward declared.

Yulia scowled. "I *am* from a farm. What do you *expect*?"

"Sorry. I didn't mean ... ."

But Yulia had switched on an ancient Ultra radio and become preoccupied with tuning in to some music.

"Can I help?" he asked, kneeling down beside her. While she struggled with the tuning knob, he lifted her hand from her knee and kissed the back of it softly.

When he opened his eyes, she turned to smile at him and murmured:

"You know what this means?"

Yulia led him to the bedroom while Debussy's Clair de Lune crackled out of the tiny speaker. She waited until Edward lay beside her on the bed and cupped his elbow delicately. The gesture almost seemed to impart a magical energy, propelling his hand to alight on her shoulder. He saw acceptance in her brown eyes and drew in a deep, primeval breath, before sliding his hand down to the shallow valley of her waist, soon forgetting the faint whisper of music.

"I can't believe I am touching you," he whispered.

"Why?"

"Ask me the question again; the one you asked earlier."

"What? Am I beautiful?"

"You are the most beautiful woman I have ever seen."

***

"Are you really married?" Yulia asked, in answer to Edward's compliment.

"I told you, yes!"

"But in Russia men often take off their ring to seduce women. Is it the same here?"

"Yes! I suppose so!" He laughed. "But not me! I'm wearing mine. Look!"

"Men are the same everywhere! And women, I suppose. Did you have many girlfriends when you were young?"

Yulia wriggled closer to Edward and placed her soft lips against his. He eagerly kissed her and felt a great attractive energy rising from his loin, pulling him toward her body. He eased his hips against hers and wrapped his arms around her. Yulia giggled and pulled away, exclaiming:

"Do women kiss like this in England? It seems very ... bold and yet gentle!"

"Oh, sorry."

"No. It's fine. Don't be embarrassed. *I* am sorry. It just surprised me. Men don't kiss like this in Russia; at least no men kissed *me* like that."

She rolled onto her back, so Edward lay down and placed his hands on his stomach. It seemed as if they had eternity to themselves.

"What was your question again?" Edward asked.

"I can't remember. Something about your childhood. Tell me more. I like to hear about it."

"Why? It was nothing special."

"My childhood wasn't much, and it was cut short ... ."

"Oh? Why?"

"It doesn't matter. Tell me about yours."

She rolled to face him and curled her hand into a delicate fist on his chest while smiling at him. Her eyes revealed a girlish eagerness that drew Edward into her world and completely overcame him, so that he felt like the luckiest man alive.

"You intimidated me slightly in the bar," Edward said. "I wanted to protect you, but you had that executive under complete control! I mean; it was marvellous, in a way, but I'm not used to that kind of confidence in a woman. I'm sure *he's* quite shocked too!"

"Oh. Do you think I overdid it?" she asked, giggling.

"No. No, I don't think so. I wanted him to go. But at any rate, here we are! Safe and sound!"

"Yes. It's been fun, so far!"

"Jolly good, I'd say!"

"Jolly good! Ha! Do people still say that? Don't try *too* hard. I am always shy with strangers."

Edward dismissed the temptation to ask if she still considered him a stranger, but it wasn't so easy for him to dismiss his childish use of 'jolly good.' He suddenly felt naked, catapulted back to a tranquil and less self-conscious England of the 1930s. Putting his hand behind his head, he dreamed up another version of his childhood. This time he talked for pleasure, making it as near poetry as he could manage, but he still tried to shield his own insecurities from her penetrating mind:

***

"I remember the time my sister, Suzy, fell out of a tree, into some stinging nettles – you know; those green leaves with little hairs that sting so much. Do you have them in Russia?"

"Oh yes."

"We had a pretty German nanny, Brigitte. She told me she didn't know about the stinging nettles, because she grew up in a city, Hamburg. We traipsed – sorry, walked – back to the lodge in single file. I walked behind Brigitte and when she half-stumbled, I reached out and held her waist in both my hands. I nearly died at the pleasure of it, but she didn't stop me … ."

"Died?"

"It's a saying. For – you know – being really excited, or shocked."

"Oh. I see. You remember all that so clearly!"

"It's one of those memories that really sticks in your mind. But you know, I often feel I left something behind on that holiday. But I can never think what."

"Did you? You know? When you touched Brigitte?"

"Get excited? That way? Yes. Very."

Yulia chuckled. "Go on. I like this story now!"

"Well that's it. Apart from one other thing … ."

"What?"

"About a day before we came home, I caught a glimpse of her washing, through a crack in the washroom door. She stood naked to the waist! I even saw her turn slightly. It really excited me!"

"That actually happened?"

"Yeah!"

Yulia stared into Edward's eyes for a long time before declaring, "No! I don't believe that last bit. You're lying!"

Edward tried to brazen it out, but knew he had been cornered. "Okay. Yes. It's a lie. I never saw that."

"It was a very good lie," Yulia said, to console him.

"I was taught by the best, my father. Well, I learned by observation!"

Edward suddenly tasted burnt treacle in his mouth. He searched his memory and remembered his father persuading them that he could cook, but then burning the food.

"You're not angry for me for lying?" he asked.

"Oh no. I am flattered." Yulia wriggled closer and put her hand on his breast. "Your heart is beating fast. Must be that thought!"

"Maybe." Edward frowned.

Yulia quickly added, "I never thought you would be a good liar. My mother said, 'The only thing uglier than the truth is a badly told lie.'"

"Your mum must be quite a woman!"

"Um. She gave me a lot of other advice, about covering weaknesses with something bold. Look, I have ugly feet!" She suddenly raised her legs and waggled her feet in the air. "Can't you see I have thick ankles? Far too thick. That's why I wore the red shoes!"

"The only reason?"

Yulia slapped his chest playfully and continued:

"She also told me that her advice was for me only. 'Men's truth,' she said, 'must be different to ours. Never tell Demitri the advice I give to you.'"

"Who's Demitri?"

"My little brother."

"Hm! You're far too clever to be just a secretary. You must be a spy! Are you?"

"Let's play a little game. For ten questions, I will tell you a lie, or the truth. But I won't tell you which. It will be the same for all of them. But I can refuse to answer. For each question that I answer, I can ask you a question and you have to tell the truth"

"Hm. Alright. Are you from Russia?"

"No answer!"

"You're just making this up! This seems unfair! Is red your favourite colour?"

"No. Now my turn. Do you love your wife?"

"Oh great! Well, yes, I guess I still do, but less each year … each week in fact! Ha!"

"Good. Next question!"

"Is Bregovsky your lover?"

"No. Do you love me?"

"Hm. I don't know. It's too soon to tell."

"Yes or no?"

"Hey! You can choose not to answer, so I can too!"

"Alright, I will deduct one question." She held up one hand, splaying her fingers. "You now only have five!"

"This isn't fair!"

"I am a *Russian* woman! What do you *expect*?"

"Hm… Wait! Hm. Do you like animals?"

"Hm. Sometimes. It depends … ."

"Yes or no?"

"Oh, I guess … hm … yes."

"Good."

"My question. Which part of my body do you like most?"

"Oh. I haven't seen it yet!"

"Wait. I show you." She stood next to the bed and pulled the blouse tight over her bust. Then she pulled the trousers tight around her bottom and rotated on the balls of her feet. "Now? Decide!"

"Bust, I think. It's a bit unf- ... ."

"Bust! You said it!"

Yulia folded one more finger and waved her hand to show Edward how many questions he had left.

"Do you always lie?" Edward asked.

"No."

"Hm. Until now I thought you were choosing to lie. But wait, I have an idea."

"Wait. I have a question," Yulia countered, waggling three fingers at him. "If you had to choose between me and your wife, assuming you had no children, who would you choose?"

"You. I mean ... ."

"Me! Good! Two questions left!"

Edward checked her hand and saw only two fingers. "Wait! It should be three!"

"No. You have lost count. It's now two! Trust me!"

"Damn. You may be right. I can't remember. I need to keep count too." He held up two fingers. "Do you enjoy lying?"

"Yes. Certainly, sometimes."

"Okay."

"My question. If I left now and you never saw me again, what would you do?"

"Oh. I hadn't thought of that!"

"Well, I *am* leaving on Saturday!"

"Yes. I would be sad. I think I would want to write to you, if I could get your address. But that would get me in trouble. Especially if ... . My last question?"

"Yes. Go!"

"Are you a spy?"

"Yes!"

"Oh! Now I'm totally confused. This is a silly game!"

"Maybe. I have one last question though."

"Okay. Go on."

"Please can you fetch me a glass of water from the bathroom?"

"Oh. Ha! Of course. I need to use the bathroom anyway!"

'He is getting tense,' Yulia thought. 'Remember your training in Istanbul Yulia! I must not push him.'

When Edward returned, she had unfastened three more buttons on her blouse.

"I felt hot!" she said, pouting. "That is probably why I am dehydrated. Do you mind if I open the windows? It's so hot compared with Leningrad district and Moscva!"

"You mean Moscow!"

"Yes."

Edward glanced at the windows and saw the silhouette of a tree nod in the night breeze. "Yes, it *is* a bit hot. Open them. And drink this!"

Yulia propped herself up on one elbow to take the glass of water. This left more of her cleavage available for Edward to look at. He lay down beside her to wait for her story while she finished sipping the cold water:

"I started telling you about *my* mother," she began, "so perhaps I should continue talking about my childhood! Where do I start? Hm. I was born on 24 June, 1926, in a village called Porozhek, not far to the south of Leningrad. My father was, I mean *is*, a peasant farmer and my mother helped him. They were simple people but kind, most of the time. I have one younger brother, Demitri. My childhood was very ordinary."

Edward only half listened. He began to understand that by telling her the picnic story he had been invoking some secret force, a demon in his soul. Yulia had understood the same thing instantly. She continued:

"As I said, my parents were simple and I had a curious mind, so that I wasn't close to them. My best friend was Yuri. We had to walk 10 km to school, so we rode on my father's old bicycle on the days when he didn't need it. I would be standing up and Yuri would hold on to me for his dear life! On the way home from school we would often stop and play in the fields near my village. We saw the rocket there!

"Yuri would always want to race me. Ah! Yuri! He is such a lovely soul. Soft brown curls, freckles and a sweet, smiling face! But he never beat me! He would always start slowly and then catch me up. But as he overtook me, he touched me on the shoulder like this!"

Yulia tapped Edward's shoulder lightly and giggled.

"So I would run a bit slowly and when I felt him tap, I ran faster! Ah, Yuri! How I miss those days! And the blue skies! The people from – what do you call the Nomads? Chingiz Khan and his warriors?"

"You mean Ghengis Khan? Mongols."

"Ah yes. Mongols call the place where the wide, blue sky meets Lake Baikal the Infinite Blue Heaven. It is their paradise. If you have never seen the wide sky over Russia, you must go there. It is the biggest sapphire in the Universe!

"But the forest was my best *secret* friend. Yuri didn't know it, but I had a secret place, a *very* secret place. Where I went when he wasn't with me. Inside a forest, I found a small stream, and nearby I found a very pretty flower.

"It looked so beautiful and delicate that I used to talk to it. But not like your *trees*! If it knew anything, it would not know much of men, only polar bears and mamont – what do you call it in English? The hairy elephant?"

"Oh, mammoth?"

"Yes. But it never spoke back. It sat there, looking very pretty. It was almost white, but slightly pink. Just a little bit. With a green tongue. But it would only come up for a few days and then disappear. I knew when it would appear, so I spent a lot of time there. Later, in Leningrad library, I discovered that it was an orchid. Shall I tell you a secret?"

"Yes, please!"

"It is a very *big* secret. I never told Yuri or *anybody* before. Once, on a very hot day, I took all my clothes off and lay in the stream. It was ice-cold, but I felt so *alive*! I climbed out and sunbathed on the soil and leaves. It felt so good to touch the soil with my whole body. Have you ever done that?"

"No ... . No, I can't say I have."

"Oh. Do you think it is strange? Was it wrong?"

"Oh no! I think it's terrific! I wish I had the courage to do such things."

"Oh, I'm sure you can. But English people are so *stiff upper lip*! Oh, and let me tell you another story!"

Yulia sat up suddenly, which made her breasts sway inside her blouse. Edward felt a hardness growing inside his trousers while he watched her. Yulia sat against the bed's upholstered headboard and pulled her knees up under her elbows, continuing:

"I was tall for my age and I played football with the older boys in the village. We played on some waste ground and used a pig's bladder, but it always exploded when you kicked it too hard, or punctured on stones, or barbed wire fences. But when I had my curves, the boys started to tease me and touch me. The games became chaotic and some of the boys didn't want me to play anymore. I became quite aggressive and I yelled at them to go and have sex with their aunties. Ha! But they wouldn't let me play. And some of them told their parents about me swearing and my father beat me with a stick! Only Yuri tried to protect me.

"A few weeks later, we went to visit my uncle, who lived in Tosno, the nearest town. He owns a grocery shop there and a van. Demitri and I had nothing to do, so we looked in the shops and I saw a real football, one made from leather. I begged my uncle to lend me the money to purchase it. 'What will you do to earn it?' he asked. I told him I would 'Milk all your goats for a week.' But he just laughed and told me to clean the house and barn for three days. His wife looked very pleased with the arrangement. But I worked hard for that football. My uncle drove Demitri home, so that they didn't have to feed him too. After three days, I had the football, so I returned home. I planned to keep the ball and tell only the players that I liked. I would start my own game! This is how I planned my revenge. But Yuri thought this wasn't a good idea! So instead I took my ball to the village game and they let me play! Things were okay for a few months, but then somebody punctured the ball on a barbed-wire fence. Things returned to normal and then they didn't want me to play anymore."

"Oh, that's so sad. Girls never play football here. Well, Suzy might have when we were very small … ."

"Oh. That seems sad too. Are they too weak?"

"Ha! Maybe."

"In the summer, my uncle took father and I in the van, 150 km south east, to the nearest state-run farm. They are very large! Father had been going there nearly all his life for the harvest. He told me that his grandfather came from Turkey and there is a rumour that *his* grandfather had been born in Cyprus. I used to fantasise that the family had gradually migrated north, looking for Leningrad, but had run out of money. And one day, I would go there and complete the journey! But I started the harvest story ... . Demitri had to stay behind, because it was very hard work. For two or three weeks, we slept in a barn and ate only porridge and soup with dumplings. The farm had three red tractors, which towed reaping machines. We spent all day threshing the wheat by hand. I hated it; the dust would get in your nose and ears and hair. And we couldn't wash. I often became ill, but we had to keep working hard. Father told me it would pay for our food for the winter. I met some interesting people though. Once I met a Black Russian. He came from Kazakhstan. I don't like the name Black Russian, but this is what white Russians call people from the east. They were treated even worse than us and he was paid less!

"But that is all the good things my uncle did for me ... ." Yulia paused, expecting Edward to reply, but his eyes were closed and breathing even. "Seems *so* long ago."

***

Yulia's thoughts dwelt on her uncle Makar.

About two months after he watched her milk the goat, he came to visit when Demitri was out:

"I bought you a present Yulia. I ... I wasn't feeling well last time."

"Oh. What is it?"

"Open it and see," he said, handing her a small box, wrapped in dark blue paper and tied with string.

Yulia's face broke into a broad smile when she opened the box and saw a red, silk ribbon. But then she frowned:

"Red is not really my colour. Mother says so."

"Well why don't you try it on and I will tell you what *I* think?"

"Alright."

Yulia struggled to tie the bow around her hair, as her uncle had anticipated.

"Let me help you Yulia!" he suggested, sitting on the bed behind her.

He had an idea, so tried to bounce on the straw mattress.

"This bed is not very comfortable Yulia. Would you like one filled with goose feathers?"

"Oh yes Uncle Makar! Would you buy it for me?"

"Maybe. There! Turn round and let me look!"

Yulia spun round and Makar grinned at the red ribbon now encircling a sheaf of her golden hair.

"You look pretty dear," he murmured, trying to hold her gaze of innocent joy. "Remember the goat? I can see somebody else that requires milking."

Yulia shook her head slowly, not understanding whom he meant, but Makar stretched out a hand toward her. She studied his hand as he pressed it gently against her chest, shocking her.

"No! Uncle!" she protested, pulling back beyond his reach and jumping up. He stood up and reached his great arm around her, pressing her close. She tried everything to escape his embrace, but he proved too strong. He tried to sooth her, but he seemed to be speaking too quickly, out of breath himself. She struggled with every last bit of her strength. Makar caught the tundra-snow-white fear of a trapped animal in her eyes, but it didn't stop him:

"Yulia! I'm your … uncle. Your parents know I'm up here! Everything is safe. Trust me! They won't interfere … even if you scream! See me as a friend! Please! Yulia! Stand still!"

Yulia could not organise her thoughts into any comprehension of what he wanted, or why she felt the way she did. She tried to press down the rising panic, but her breathing would only come in great gulps.

Makar remembered the spreading pink stain of blood on the snow from the first rabbit that he had shot as a boy.

"If you don't, I'm afraid your father will suffer … ." her Uncle rasped into Yulia's ear.

She wanted to scream, "*Why?*" but somehow the question died on her lips.

Yulia's muscles suddenly lost their knot-hard strength and her bucking subsided slightly. Sensing his advantage, Makar thrust his hands inside Yulia's tunic. But she didn't want to remember … .

Yulia suddenly heard Edward's voice and snapped back to the bed in the Hotel with a shocked jolt.

***

"Sorry, I fell asleep, I think." Edward mumbled. "What were you saying? Oh, about your uncle. And what came after that? You said your childhood was cut short?"

"Oh. Something happened. I might tell you another day. But seeing the rocket really changed my life. Yes … . After that, I wanted to go to Leningrad … . I wanted to get away very much! Then the Army came to my village, looking for recruits. I think it was 1940. I wanted to go; I had no fear of the state then. I was a bit too young, but they said they would come back and they did, a few months later. I went to Leningrad for the first time during that winter! I completed my education at fifteen and began my industrial education. Just after my sixteenth birthday the Nazis invaded us. I was moved far back from the frontline, to work in a factory that made parts for aero engines. They said I could become a pilot later. But because of my qualifications, Yuri was able to send me to a special conference. I can't tell you more about it, but a friend of General Bregovsky noticed me, and that's how I came to be his secretary."

"So you *are* in the NKVD?"

"Yes, and no."

"What does that mean?"

"I am just a secretary."

Yulia stared into Edward's eyes, as if trying to tell him something. A few things differed about her story from her original explanation for how she had gone to Leningrad. He guessed:

"It was the NKVD who recruited you to Leningrad, wasn't it?"

Yulia's solemn eyes stared at him for just a moment longer than he would have expected, so that he felt as if the precious gift of truth had been passed to him.

Yulia felt torn inside, both physically and emotionally, as she had done for almost as long as she could remember. But the resulting state of mind had become so ubiquitous that she no longer noticed it or thought of feeling anything else. She had developed a pragmatic approach to dealing with disappointment, and this had served her well with the NKVD. Her training had including a course on seducing men, in Istanbul, where she had learned that a woman had to get access to a man's emotions, if she wanted to make him truly fall in love with her. Only then could she extract secrets or promises to defect.

Her instructor called the technique the 'Hard Luck' story, or the 'Ugly Child.' The roots of this lesson in the NKVD were obscure. It was considered bad luck in Russia for a stranger to look at a baby, and even worse to compliment it. Instead one should say, "Oh, what an ugly child." Many old wives believed that breaking this rule led to a child truly growing up ugly, so bad luck and ugliness had somehow become entwined.

"If you want to pull on a man's heart strings," her instructor had told her, "you should tell them a bad luck story, or that you were an ugly child. Make the man feel sorry for you and you will have him eating out of your hand.

Yulia didn't even need to make up such a story, but she didn't want to use her own now, for there was another Yulia underneath the pragmatic one. She remembered that she once had a dream of a man she could trust, although it seemed a dream from her distant childhood now. One boy that she had met at Christmas had particularly haunted her. Edward seemed to encompass the last vestige of this dream. Although certainly clever, he also seemed naïve and vulnerable, but she found his vulnerability almost miraculous after her experiences with Russian men. She usually exploited men's weaknesses, if and when she located them, whereas she wanted to protect Edward's. She feared this vulnerability to be so fragile that exploiting it would damage him and remove forever his trust in her, a trust that she needed.

Besides, the Yulia that had been asleep for so long still had one other fear about Edward. She knew she liked him, but would there be a real physical attraction, a chemistry, between them? She decided to tell him a very small 'Ugly Child' story:

"I *wanted* to continue studying engineering at a university, but it quickly became obvious that there would be a price to pay for the grades I wanted. My lecturers all tried everything to get me into bed and I was stubborn. So, when I had the offer to work for Bregovsky, I took it."

"Oh. Sorry!"

Edward twisted round and kissed her vermillion lips.

But Yulia withdrew her hand, leaving Edward feeling cold, confused. He whispered:

"Beauty can corrupt men's hearts."

"But my beauty is *not part of me*! I wish you would see me as an ordinary girl! In fact, I'm not *all* beautiful …"

"Oh, but you are!"

"You don't know … me."

"I want to free you," Edward whispered.

"We are both engineers. Perhaps we should build a bridge over beauty together."

They held hands again and Yulia raised his high above them.

"No, I want to *overcome* beauty!" he whispered.

"But it will be better if we can overcome beauty together." They both looked at their hands and she added, "The *touch* of *Angels*"

"Hm."

"Screaming Angels," Yulia said, flushing deep red.

Edward relaxed his arm and both hands came down to fall across Yulia's chest. She raised his and kissed it, giggling.

"Who gave you the ring?" Edward asked.

"This?" she replied, turning a ring with a white stone around her finger. "My husband, Yuri."

"Oh."

***

It was 2 am. Derby's smoggy scowl winked silently outside the window. Only the occasional creak of a settling wall could be heard above the whispers inside Suite 36.

"Russian men are so brutal," Yulia whispered, summoning Edward back from the precipice of sleep. "You are so gentle, unlike other men. I may be beautiful, but Russian men don't respect it. They don't trust it and treat beautiful women like witches. I think they try to beat something out of us. But ... ."

"What?"

"Nothing."

"Hm. Well Bregovsky does."

"What?"

"Respect beauty."

"Perhaps, sometimes ... ."

"Are you his mistress?"

"Ha! No! I am his secretary, but that has a different meaning in Soviet Union."

"I don't think I can do this," Edward replied, suddenly rolling off the bed and standing up.

"Oh, you think you are so clean! So holy! You have no idea how tough life is in Soviet Union. Men make all the rules and women don't break them!" She sat up and got off the bed, adding, "If they want to live!" Edward could see spit fly from her mouth and felt shocked by her vehemence. He sat down again while she strode around the room, waving her arms:

"Okay, so my uncle was bad to me, but *you* are no better! All men are the same!"

"Hey! Wait a *minute* ... !"

But Yulia collapsed over the bed, sobbing into her arms and cutting off Edward's protest. He took hold of her shaking shoulders, whispering:

"Come on darling. I'm *not* like *that*."

Yulia knew she had actually lost control, so didn't answer at first. She harboured a guilt about the rape. Not only had it damaged her confidence, but undermined her control over emotions when she allowed herself to think about it. She struggled to control an anger that rose higher and higher. Neither the anger not guilt would subside.

"I hate my body," she told herself. "I wish I was ugly. All over!"

Edward wanted to laugh, but Yulia stared him down coldly. She had barely stopped herself spitting out her greatest secret. Besides her thick ankles, Yulia had one other physical fault, one that not even her family in Porozhek knew about. On her lower back, she had a birthmark, small at first, but which had since grown to the size of her hand. On the only occasion that she had been able to use two mirrors to look at it, she thought it looked like a frog. She felt so ashamed of it that she had felt some small relief after the rape, relief that at least her uncle had not seen the scar. Shuddering, she sat up.

Edward wiped the tears from her eyes, led her round to lay on the bed beside him and entwined her within his limbs. He held on to her until her sobbing became weeping and at last, silence. When her grinning, reddened face emerged from his breast, she kissed him lightly, murmuring:

"Thank you."

"What for?"

"Being here. I feel so much better."

Yulia wiped her eyes and noticed Edward's eyes on her cleavage, so she whispered:

"Don't!"

"What?"

"Look away."

She reached for his hand, but Edward reached out and cupped her breast. He fondled it for a while and then peeled her blouse off her raised shoulder. Yulia raised her arm and wriggled out of the blouse. While he caressed her breasts Yulia struggled with the knot in his blue tie.

"Oh, I can't do it!" she declared, giggling.

"Ha! Ha! Sorry."

"Russian men don't wear them. Not normally, anyway."

Edward removed his tie, shirt and white vest within moments, pressed against her and ran his hands down the smooth, downy furrow of her back.

"Yes!" Yulia whispered. She shuddered as Edward nibbled her ear and kissed the tiny hairs on her neck.

Edward felt himself stiffen, so he unfastened the brass buckle of his leather belt and hauled down his working trousers. He hardly noticed Yulia shimmy out of her own trousers.

"Did you hear that?" Yulia gasped.

Edward couldn't remove his gaze from her heaving rib cage, but he tried to listen:

"I can't hear anything darling."

"I'm just a bit shy. That's all."

Yulia snuggled closer to him, but Edward's hardness subsided as his shorts rustled against her silk knickers. He kissed her more ardently and she responded, but then he pulled his lips away, whispering:

"I can't."

"Oh."

Edward quickly stood up and began to dress.

"What's wrong?" Yulia asked.

"I don't know! I'm sorry." He shook his head in disbelief. "This has never happened before!"

"That's a ... false excuse!" she yelled, jumping up.

'Oh no, here we go again!' he thought. 'She's either *very* highly-strung, or acting.'

"Just because you probably had a hard time with some woman," she continued, "you feel low and blame that on my beauty, which I hate by the way!"

"No. Seriously. I mean it!"

"Oh Edward, I don't believe it! You wouldn't make love to me if I was ugly, would you? *Would* you?"

"No. I mean yes. I mean. I think I have to go!"

"But will you tell them about me? If anything happened, it wasn't my fault!"

"Explain it then!"

"Sit down then!"

Edward sat down as if he had been punched in the stomach. Yulia, however, stood up and paced, trying to organise her thoughts. As she talked, she waved her arms wildly:

"You are right; Kirill recruited me *just* for this trip, although I didn't know it at the time. Even Yuri kept secrets from me! Kirill spent of a lot of time training me to observe, so that I could make notes later. He was very clever, telling me that the mission would be to gather as much intelligence about British production methods as possible. I overheard him asking somebody, 'Are the shoes ready?' very early on, but only a few days before we left did he say that I had wear new, red shoes. He had already told me that I had to try and walk around as many lathes as possible, to distract the Rolls Royce workers, so that Kirill and his agents could take photographs. I thought the shoes were only another trick to distract stupid English men!" She hoped her little lie would be lost in the volley of truths she had fired at Edward. "From what you are telling me, I suspect this wasn't the case ... ." She made a moue at Edward and stood stock still.

Edward didn't completely believe her story, but he believed her to be innocent, and yet his head swirled with emotions that he didn't understand. He needed time to think.

"Oh, come on and sit down," he told her. "It's so late. I'm too tired to argue any more. I need to think about this tomorrow."

Yulia thought about asking him to apologise, but felt too guilty to try.

"Don't go back to *your room. Please!*" she begged.

Edward lay beside her. His thoughts hovered over such perilous depths as he had never imagined, before sleep finally whispered its sweet invitation and took him into her arms.

Yulia closed her eyes, hating herself.

Chapter Three

*B*eetle on white window sill. So small, shimmering blue. Will it fall? No. Too wise. Clanking, cruddy morning outside window. Why didn't she pull the curtains? Plume of black smoke. Steam train?

"Toot! Toot!"

There's the whistle. Must be a train. Ah yes, Derby!

Edward's rambling thoughts coalesced into one question:

What day is it?

"Tuesday," he replied to his own question. He checked his watch:

"7.41."

Edward wearily propped himself up on his elbows and peered out of the window, licking his furry tongue into some kind of eel-like, lubricious usefulness. He did a quick visual check; both he and Yulia were still wearing underpants.

"So nothing happened," he told himself.

But his thoughts still hammered against each other, leaving him with no substantial thought to communicate.

He decided to leave, but when he eased off the bed, the Russian beauty next to him stirred.

"Are you going?" she mumbled.

"Yes. I have to have a bath and go to work. I'll see you later. Don't worry ... ."

Yulia rolled over and shielded her eyes from the dawn light with her hand. Her face crinkled up with irritation, which only strummed Edward's heart strings harder.

"I'm not!" she added. "But I had better sleep or Yu- ... , I mean Kirill, will kill me."

There seemed no answer to that, so Edward picked up his discarded clothes and padded to her door. Taking one last look, he took in her long legs, curled beneath her silk knickers, and the shadow of her belly inside her dishevelled blouse. He felt an ache in his gut.

"Good bye!" he murmured, and closed the door.

Edward felt grateful for the mundane routines that would get him to his office without having to think. A cold fear lurked below all other concerns, but there were so many confusing thoughts that he kept telling himself he would have to get to the fear when he sorted out the others.

He shaved, took a bath and put on fresh clothes before calling room service for breakfast and a copy of The Times. While he waited, he sat, watching Derby wake through his own grimy window. On impulse, he unfastened and pulled up the sash to feel the crisp air, but quickly slammed it down when the noise assailed his eardrums. He paced around the room.

'I could get hanged for this, if I fail to report my suspicions. It *could* be called treachery. No! That's madness. I haven't done anything wrong! I just have to work her out, where her loyalties lie. Does she love me? Probably not yet. I'm not that naïve! Maybe she has been trained to do this. *Maybe* that's why they brought her!'

The ice-cold thought forced him to sit down on the bed again and stare at the wall. His thoughts quickly became a miasma of wormy demons, struggling to strangle each other in their struggle for dominance. Only with the greatest of self-will did he force some order into his unruly head:

'But wait! That look in her eye? She was admitting to being a spy. She must care about me. I have to believe that. God! All I wanted to do was save my job and perhaps get promoted! Look at me!'

A light tap sounded on the door and a waiter bought in a large tray, laden with his breakfast and paper. Edward tried to read the first few pages, but found he could only manage the smaller columns of news. People in Tewkesbury were up in arms about the newly introduced rationing of bread for the first time in British history. Children were no longer to be allowed to visit farms during school time. And the porter had been found guilty of murdering Cornelius Collins by setting fire to the Berkeley hotel in Worthing.

Edward wiped the boiled egg yolk from his lips, swigged down the last dregs of the lukewarm tea and tied on his shoes.

Slinging his coat and hat on, he picked up his brief case and sat in reception to wait for the limousine, which he knew would be bang on time at 9 am.

***

The executive, who had harangued Yulia in the bar, sat in the limousine, working his jaw muscles to control a hangover. Mikoyan sat on the front passenger seat, clearly on his way to visit Hooker. Two other Rolls executives read their copies of The Times and The Daily Telegraph, sparing Edward any conversation other than a peremptory "Good morning."

He glanced, out of curiosity, at the area of floor where Yulia had first sat. To his surprise and delight, he saw three metallic glints there.

"Like diamonds!" he reflected.

Suddenly he knew exactly what he had to do, so pulled out his wallet and inspected it, as if checking its contents. Replacing it he stared out of the window until the limousine reached the factory. He followed the others out of the car, but then turned back, saying:

"It must have fallen out of my pocket!"

Edward barely reached the car before the chauffeur drove off.

"Wait!" he shouted. "I think I lost something!"

Sitting on the back seat, he pretended to be looking for the 'something' on the floor while wrapping the three metal shavings in his handkerchief and pocketing it.

Edward headed straight for his office, a small space that had been separated from the main workshop by the thinnest partition, to mark his status as a white-collar worker. He feared a memo telling him to leave the Russian girl alone, or that the Secret Service would be talking to him, but saw with relief the absence of anything on his blotter. The cold knot in the pit of his stomach eased, so he sat down and took his spare pair of spectacles from the case in his drawer.

"A'right Arry! Drop it there!" a Cockney voice yelled, a fraction of a second before the clanging sound of steel, dropping onto steel, reverberated around the workshop.

"Mary," Edward called down the office telephone. "Bring me a strong cup of tea, would you?"

"Certainly Mister Torrens. The usual sugars?"

"No. Two today. I have a bit of a hangover."

Edward had little to do during the Russian delegation's visit, except organise the production and duplication of blue prints for the Nene engine, and the packing of ten engines with their spares, ready to leave for London on the Saturday. A meeting with the staff assigned to him had been set for 10 am. Until then, he idly turned over the pages of a report, which he had been preparing, about production costs of the Nene's successor. He felt no urgency about the matter and had no will at all to focus on it, so he sipped his tea.

"Reassuringly bland and bitter."

Thinking about why seemed a welcome distraction:

'Bitter, because of the tannin-black interior of an urn that had never been cleaned, and bland, because of the habit of the maids to add more water to the half-pound of tea-leaves, rather than replace them during the day.'

Edward flattered himself that he could reason out problems with the best. He set himself to analysing Yulia and suddenly found himself reaching for his breast pocket. But he glanced at his watch as an afterthought and saw the minute hand reach the number twelve. He pulled his hand away from his pocket, just as his project staff filed silently through his open door and stood around his desk.

"Okay then!" he began. "Are we up to speed on the blue prints? Humphrey?"

"I think so. We should be finished tomorrow or Thursday, at the latest."

"Good. And the packing. Don? How's your team doing?"

Edward tried to avoid making direct eye-contact with any of his men for more than the briefest moment, knowing this to be irrational, but fearing that his guilt would show.

"We're a bit behind Ed. We found that the crates aren't big enough for the ten of your spare expansion chambers that Lucas told us would fit. I *think* this is because somebody forgot to account for the late addition of a longer bracket. We've been faffin' around every way to get them in, but we can only fit eight. That means I have to order another two crates!"

Don exaggerated his exasperation, a theatrical touch that he knew would go down well with Edward and counter any temptation to criticise the packing team.

"I knew it!" Edward replied. "I said we should take one engine apart and pack the whole lot in a large crate. That way we would *know* how many crates we needed. Letting contractors tell us was *not* wise!"

Even Edward pulled his punches, not saying what he really thought of senior Rolls Royce management. His indignation brought knowing nods and smiles from his teams, but with less enthusiasm than he expected.

"I'll call Lucas," he continued, "and make sure that this doesn't happen again and that they pay for the crates. Anything else?"

A lot of grim faces refused to make eye-contact with Edward, so he concluded the meeting with some extra enthusiasm:

"Great! You all know what's to be done. We'll meet again, same time, tomorrow."

Alone again, Edward sat down heavily, reached for his breast pocket and took out his leather wallet and spectacles case. He opened the wallet at a compartment containing his only photograph of Ewa, grainy, black and white, torn on one corner, and placed it on end, like a book. Putting on his spectacles, Edward's eyes bored into his icon, but no affection for his past life would come. Only when he closed his eyes and remembered Ewa's clear, soprano voice did he feel a pang of guilt, which seemed to echo through his gut to his eyes and almost made him cry.

Edward had stumbled from one exotically named woman to another in his adult love life. When he reflected on this it became apparent that he no longer trusted women from his own country.

Compared with Brigitte's sharp intellect and yet gentle nature, the girls he spoke to at school, and later in London, seemed somehow distant and vague. Try as he might, he could not fathom what they wanted from him. He seemed to constantly disappoint them, and they him.

However, one girl at school had caught his attention. Edward joined the choir, so that he could stand behind Shelley and lean forward when everyone else concentrated on singing, so that his nose penetrated her brown locks, those gossamer veils of her boudoir. He felt sure that she knew what he did and this excited him more, but he never had the courage to tell her how he felt, because he feared that she would slough off the magic that he had spun around her in his mind. She would turn out to be an ordinary girl, with ordinary appetites, and he didn't want the object of his secret desire to be less than perfect.

Shelley's lithe body and shy intelligence reminded him of something, a distant dream of his early childhood. It seemed to have something to do with the Bailiff's lodge, but when he thought about that, he either saw Brigitte, or a darkness, where his mother should have been.

Edward's feelings about women were confused, so much so that he envied his younger brother for a crudeness that he couldn't match.

"I saw Julia Smith's blue knickers today!" Sam would happily recount with a dirty grin.

This would make Edward withdraw more completely within himself, disappointing Sam, who only wanted to share a pleasure with his older brother.

Ewa had been the one exception to Edward's abstinence from English women. Gay and intelligent, but in a feminine and home-loving way, she had warmed his heart and stolen his soul. Openly telling him that she only wanted a safe home and a husband that she could trust, her needs seemed simple, so that Edward could understand her. Ewa didn't seem to have ambitions for wealth or a career of her own and put more emphasis on happiness and love than the other English women he knew. But above all, she had been honest to her core.

Edward had slowly become aware of something else about himself; that he distanced himself from his own emotions and placed greater trust on what he could see. Colours and textures seemed to give him a better representation of real life, and his true goal, beyond a vague love of God, had been the pursuit of light, a pure light that he had almost forgotten.

But his love of beauty had led him to make his biggest mistake. Viktoria had learned all the lessons her mother could teach her about bewitching men, and not for any good purpose, but for personal ambition. Edward had only seen this too late, after he had married her. And now it seemed that his complete trust of beauty had led him astray again.

"God, I must forget this Russian woman. She will end my career, and possibly my life! I must be mad!"

Edward smiled at his recent foolishness and let peace settle over him. He took up his report and managed to reach page three before the ghost of Yulia passed in front of his inner eye. Then the telephone rang.

"Yes sir," Edward answered. "Alright, I'll be there in five minutes."

Edward sat down gingerly in the red, leather chair that Sanderson had pulled back from the desk for him. Sanderson had never offered him a chair before, so Edward's heart thumped out the rhythm of his own terror as he swallowed, smiled and tried to look calm and relaxed.

"I called you here Edward," his boss began, "about a tricky issue. Now, you know how important this whole Russian ... *thing* ... is and you know the powers-that-be are behind it. So, I don't want you to stop being friendly. You have done great job so far and your answer at the dinner table last night was exemplary, so Stanley Hooker tells me. Just the right amount of ... *formalité*! But I have been asked to warn you not to spend *too* much time with the young Russian *woman*. Don't trust her! I know it's probably innocent and none of our business – after all, she *is* a *very* attractive woman and I wouldn't mind being in your shoes! Just ease off a bit, eh? A romance there cannot have any future. And it's very dangerous. People will *talk*!"

Edward had little doubt that the disgruntled executive had reported his liaison. He also knew that Stanley Hooker must have told Sanderson to ease off on him. There could be no other reason for Sanderson's friendly approach. Edward tried not to sound angry:

"Definitely sir."

"Good! Good!" his boss said, standing up and gesturing with an open hand toward the door.

Edward stood and swung on the balls of his feet.

"Would you like a round of golf next week?" Sanderson asked.

An invitation to play gold might be the first sniff of promotion to the upper echelons of Rolls Royce that an executive could get, but Edward knew that the real message was:

Do this our way and you will get promotion. Mess it up more and it will mean your job.

"I can assure you sir," he interjected. "My interest is *strictly* professional."

"Good! Good! I thought as much. How are your two projects going?"

The door shut in Edward's face only a moment after he replied:

"Fine sir. I have no problem with that."

***

Edward's belly could not contain food during that particular lunchtime, so he drank another cup of tea, visited the Men's Room and decided to take a stroll around the factory grounds. For most of the perimeter, this amounted to stepping between, or over, broken pallets, and walking down narrow passageways between fences and the factory walls, but on one side lay a cricket pitch, a grassed open space and a narrow causeway, which led to two tennis courts. The borders of the open space had been planted with a few, pink rhododendrons. Edward liked to go there when the sun was out and he had a lot on his mind. Sometimes, if he had built up the right rhythm, when he came to the open space he felt his thoughts expand and new ideas or solutions appeared. His lap took in the open space, the cricket pitch and the tennis courts.

"Yulia! Yulia!" he chanted. "But what of your astonishing beauty? Oh, why, when the one chance I have to relieve myself of my grief, do I find a love irresistible to the heart, but a plague to my mind? Can I have you without losing everything?"

Don ran up to Edward in his sports kit, his calves rippling oak knots.

"Want a game of tennis Ed?"

"Nah! Thinking!"

"Later then? Maybe after work? Just twenty minutes?"

"No. Thanks Don."

"I guess you're too busy faffin' that Russian bird. Mind Edward. Nobody trusts her. She's a Russian. It's all around the shop!"

"You talk as if she's a witch!"

"'Appen she is!"

Edward bit his lip and said no more. But he felt like somebody had just encased him in steel. His muscles tensed, making it hard to walk.

"You're *alright* with Delores!" he yelled, twisting to face the disappearing Don.

"Oh sure! Live like a *virgin*! When you have kids, all that goes out of the window. But I'm champion."

"Okay. Take care Don."

Edward continued along the causeway. Don had stopped to watch his receding back and shouted:

"Another Engine test! 3 pm! Sanderson's orders! Sithee!"

"Alright!"

But the news of another engine test disconcerted Edward. He soon found his analytical mind trying to unravel this new mystery:

'Why would Sanderson order another test when we have already started dismantling the MK.3? Unless it's on Test Bed 2 with the latest MK.3. But *that* test bed hasn't been used yet. They only shifted prototype engine testing to Derby from Barnoldswick a few weeks ago. In fact, they're still transferring, so the facilities aren't yet up to scratch!'

The new test made Edward feel uncomfortable, so he quickened his pace.

***

As Edward had guessed, the engine test took place on Test Bed 2 and its purpose quickly became apparent. After Don and the team had finished setting everything up, Sanderson strolled in with Yulia on his arm. Edward couldn't be sure if Sanderson wanted to impress Yulia, or not, but her mischievous grin when he caught her eye told him why *she* had come.

"I asked Mister Hooker if I could see an engine test and Mister Sanderson told him it would be no problem," Yulia whispered, as soon as they were close enough. "You look cute with glasses!"

"But the Stand isn't really ready yet! It's dangerous. I wish you hadn't asked."

"Oh! Sorry! People are watching us. Let's talk about it later."

Edward filled in the form and checked the master door lock seal hadn't been tampered with. He and Don exchanged knowing glances, Don's turning to a scowl. Edward detected a hint of anger when he nodded to his friend and Don said:

"Start her up! Two thousand RPM."

This time Edward remembered to put his spectacles in their case, and tucked that inside his jacket pocket.

"I'll be back later my dear," Sanderson said, touching the elbow of Yulia's black dress.

'No point us *all* dying for your stupid whim,' Edward thought, after Sanderson had left.

As Edward ordered each incremental revolution speed increase, the engine's whistle became an ear-splitting shriek.

He had to lean close to Don's ear to yell, "Full power!" but nobody heard him whisper, "God help us!"

The engine on the Bed had standard rotor blades, which would prove a blessing. The engine held together as its pitch reached a deafening banshee wail. The ground trembled under their feet and the walls flexed, so that the listeners' ear drums compressed rhythmically, causing slight nausea and dizziness. Even so, Yulia felt ecstatic and leaned forward to touch Edward's elbow. She grinned at him and mouthed:

"It's fantastic!"

Edward grinned back, but then caught the look in the eyes of all his men, looks he had never seen before. They hated Yulia and despised him. Or was it the other way around?

He ordered Don to cut power and Yulia yelled at the top of her voice:

"I have never been so close to a jet engine going before!"

"Well? What do you think?"

"It's like magic! I love it! I want to be a pilot!"

"Ha! We don't train them here!"

Don and his team wrapped up the test while Edward led Yulia back to Sanderson's office.

"It's so loud!" she exclaimed. "Yuri and I used to call them Screaming Angels!"

"Yes, but why did you come?" Edward whispered in her ear.

"It's funny, isn't it? Witches are thought of as Evil, but wizards are worshipped like gods! Like you!"

"I'm no wizard."

"But you *are* Edward!"

"Anyway, stop avoiding the question. Why did you come?"

"I wanted to see what you did!" she replied innocently.

Edward felt like arguing that it seemed like interfering, but she looked so happy that he couldn't bear to reproach her.

"Okay. Will I see you tonight?" he added, as he left her at Sanderson's door.

"Probably! Who knows?"

She touched his elbow lightly as she sped away on black high-heels.

The danger of being with her, added to her beauty, excited Edward, so that his loins felt on fire. He couldn't wipe the grin from his face and he didn't want to.

***

Sanderson unexpectedly let Edward leave the factory at the earlier time of 4 pm and he felt on cloud nine. He had no more questions; he wanted to be with Yulia and that was *all* he wanted.

"I'm going to save her!"

Just before leaving, he opened his spare spectacle case and placed the folded handkerchief that contained the three shavings inside. Tearing off a corner of paper, he scrawled: 'Found on the Daimler floor, under the red shoes of the blonde.'

He looked for the black limousine, but it wasn't there. After thirty minutes, he shrugged his shoulders and headed for the main gates, intending to walk to the Midland Hotel. A 'Toot! Toot!' turned his head.

"Want a lift?" Don yelled, pushing open the passenger door of his little Austin 7.

"Well ... I was going to walk, but if you're asking ... ?"

"Hop in."

Don wove the little car expertly between the Derby traffic, asking:

"So what's the Midland like? Champion food?"

"Not bad. Where are you staying?"

"They have us in a boarding house. Food reminds me of the Army ... ."

"Oh."

"In Libya."

"Oh. That bad?"

"Aye. But we'll be flitting down here in a few weeks. I guess you'll be glad to be away from Barnoldswick? Closer to the action?"

"Yes."

"You're not saying much. Summat wrong?"

"No … ."

"Mind that bitch."

"Who? Yulia?"

"If that's her name. The blonde. Everyone expects the Russkies to try summat."

"You think so?"

Edward stared at the sparse dash for a moment before looking Don straight in the eye:

"Don. We've known each other a while. You're the only person I really trust here." Don stared straight through the flat windscreen. "If I tell you something, you won't question it?"

"I dunno mate. If it's against company rules … ."

"Listen, I *do* suspect something, but Sanderson has my hands tied. I have to investigate it myself. That's partly why I spend time with the girl." Don stared ahead. "In my desk drawer there is a spare spectacle case. If anything happens to me, there is something important there."

"But you should let on ta Hooker! Or somebody. Sanderson's a bastard. Don't risk yourself for nowt. Even tell somebody official … . I dunno … ."

"*They are* involved Don."

The two men stared into each other's eyes. Don pursed his lips, replying:

"Alright mate I didn't know tha' were a secret agent!"

"I'm not. Drop me here. I can walk."

"It's okay. We're nearly there."

"I'd rather not risk anyone seeing us together, especially the Russians."

"Oh."

Don stopped the car and Edward walked the rest of the way.

After bathing he changed into a fresh shirt and tapped on Yulia's door, full of nervous excitement.

"Wait!" he heard her yell.

She opened the door, wearing the same bathrobe and a towel around her hair:

"I knew it was you. Come in."

Standing on tiptoes, she kissed him, before following into her Suite and adding:

"I just took a bath and ordered food from room service. Do you want me to include something for you?"

"Well, I *am* hungry. But ... ."

"Oh stop being so polite. Rolls Royce are paying for everything. Let me be extravagant."

"Fine. You have been snooping then?"

"Ha! A girl gets nosy. Please forgive me while I dry my hair and get ready. I'm a bit late."

"Are you going out?"

Yulia picked up the telephone and held her finger up to silence Edward.

"Yes," she said into the mouthpiece. "It's Suite 36. Can I add to the order for food I just made? Edward, what would you like?"

"Sandwiches? Cheese and pickle?"

"Cheese and pickled sandwiches please. And tea and some of that nice cake with the pink icing. Thank you."

"Thank you. Where are you going?"

"You too. I hear we are all invited to London for a cabaret."

"Oh. I didn't know. Nobody told *me*."

"Oh. I don't know. Perhaps we can check. We can ask Mister Hooker when he gets here. Do you have the right clothes?"

"No. Don't worry. I really don't care. It's you I wanted to see."

"As she moved from bedroom to lounge and back again, drying her hair with the towel and painting her nails between questions, Edward could not take his eyes from her. Her skin seemed to glisten and looked completely out of place in dirty Derby."

"You look like a Hollywood film star!" he exclaimed, when she passed very close to him.

He reached out and touched the nape of her neck, relishing the tease of wet tresses on his fingers. Yulia inclined her head so that her cheek brushed his wrist. Without warning they were in each other's arms and devouring each other with kisses, but a knuckle rapped on the door, announcing:

"Room Service!"

The waiter's sly glance as he left made Edward surge with excited pride and his loins began to burn with a desire he could not hold back. Taking the tray and placing it on a table, he followed Yulia to the bedroom door and gripped her hips.

"Not now darling!" she retorted, closing the door.

By the time she emerged, immaculately dressed in a purple version of the white, ladder-back dress, matching slippers and button earrings, he had scoffed down the sandwiches and cake and washed them down with the whole contents of a tea pot.

"You look fantastic!" he mumbled, with his mouth full.

"Thank you." She looked at the lamb cutlet and cake she had ordered and added, "I'm really not that hungry. Eat the lamb, if you are not coming. I will just eat this!"

She scooped a hollow out of the fluffy sponge cake and placed the morsel on the tip of her tongue, giggling like a school girl.

"Don't they have cake in Russia?"

"No! Almost never!"

She completed dressing with the addition of a silver chain bracelet and pendant necklace, set with a purple stone. Edward could see that somebody had spent a lot of money on her clothes. Sitting in front of a large dressing table mirror she expertly piled her hair onto her head and when she was satisfied, pinned it in place, leaving a few golden wisps hanging over her ears. The effect was dazzling, but at the same time careless and contrived, reminding Edward of nothing less than a Princess who had fallen out of a haystack.

"Do I look alright?" she asked, spinning to face him.

"*I* think so. I don't see how anybody else could see otherwise."

"Oh, but Kirill is *so* fussy. Now, fasten me please."

She turned away again and pointed to four unfastened buttons below the straps of her dress with a varnished nail.

Edward stepped close to her and began fastening the first button in its cotton loop, his fingers brushing the downy hairs on the ridges either side of her spine. She quivered, so that he could not resist placing his palm against her pale skin. Yulia eased back against him, so he slid his other hand through the opening in her dress. Her slim waist left inviting spaces inside the dress, so his hands dove into them to hold her.

His breaths came quick and heavy against the nape of her neck and when he pressed his lips to kiss, she sighed, reaching above her head for his hair.

But his need made an involuntary move forward, pressing his hips against her and forcing her to bend over and lean on the dressing table.

"Oh Edward!" she whispered. "I ... I ... ."

Withdrawing his hands from her secret recesses, he reached round and pressed the front of her dress against her stomach.

But again, somebody rapped on the door:

"Yulia! Ty gotova?" called the familiar voice of Bregovsky.

Yulia spun round, so Edward pulled his arms clear, but Yulia put hers around his neck and drew him close for one, long, final kiss. She released him and strode to the door, whispering:

"It's very good that I didn't put on my lipstick yet."

She winked at Edward before letting Kirill in.

The two men eyed each other warily.

"Two minutes Kirill," she said. "I just have to put on some lipstick and then I am ready!"

To Edward's surprise, Kirill looked away first and turned to leave, shouting:

"I will wait for you in the lobby Yulia! Hurry!"

Yulia emerged from the bathroom a few minutes later, wearing lipstick that matched her dress, and touched Edward lightly on the chin with the tip of her index finger.

"Who is your worker who joked with you during the engine test?" she asked.

"Who? Oh, Don? He and I are good friends."

"Is that wise with one of your workers?"

Edward felt that he had revealed too much and furrowed his brows.

"We play football together."

"Oh."

"Look, I know what you have done with those alloy shavings. You need to give them back to me, or else I will not be able to protect you."

"Protect me? Against what?"

Yulia took a packet from her bead-encrusted handbag and stuck a cigarette in her mouth. Igniting its end with a silver lighter, she leaned against the door frame.

"Mikoyan," Edward continued. "I know he treats you badly. So does Kirill, I expect." She seemed to take too long to consider his point, so he continued, "We picked up shavings from the bottom of the car."

"You don't know how tough my life has been. My father used to beat me and the last few years of my childhood ... well it was *no* childhood. It was Hell! Hell! Men make *all* the rules in Russia. Didn't I tell you that? I have to *survive*! If you talk about this with *anyone*, Kirill will beat me and probably have me sent to a Gulag or killed! And then there is Yuri ... ."

"He beats you too?"

"Yes. Sometimes."

Edward had no reply to this onslaught. And yet when he looked into Yulia's eyes, he saw a softness there that belied her apparent rage.

"Listen, I have to go," She added. "My buttons. Oh, and don't forget your dinner."

She let Edward fasten her dress, pecked him on the cheek and led him out of her Suite.

***

After eating the lamb cutlet, Edward suddenly knew how tired he really was, so he put his feet up on the bed and turned on the radio.

He cursed himself for trying to force Yulia to confess, but he let the sounds of a big band soothe away his fear that he had lost her. Eventually, he managed to console himself with the thought that Yulia had admitted what he had suspected; that she was an unwilling spy and in danger.

"If I'm her knight in shining armour, then I am not going to fail my damsel!" he told himself, and immediately fell into a deep sleep.

Edward jerked awake at the sound of a loud 'bang.' Glancing at his watch, he saw a luminous 1.17 am. Voices ghosted from the darkness, dispossessed. Fearing for Yulia, he quickly changed into his pyjamas and dressing-gown and made for the communal toilet, as an excuse for passing Yulia's door. The light that reflected off the white door hurt his head, but brought his senses to a sharp focus. He heard Kirill shouting at Yulia and a bang, as of furniture overturning, followed by weeping. Grabbing the door handle, he suddenly stopped in his track; yes, he probably loved Yulia already, but he was not so stupid as to think he could take her away from Bregovsky yet. He had to wait. Releasing his grip on the handle, he padded back to his Suite with a heavy heart.

Edward tossed and turned in his bed, imagining, or hearing, the sounds of violent argument, and though he tried to ignore its terrible tow, he could not sleep until, finally, the miasma subsided.

But the ghosts did not leave Edward completely. Houses haunted by dead sheep and a woman in a long, white dress disturbed his sleep. After an hour, he jerked awake and sat up. Long lost in his memory had been the late-night arguments of his mother and father after that last summer holiday at the big house. He hadn't told Yulia that it was his mother's last summer on Earth. Her illness quickened over the previous summer and with approaching death, came deep despair in her husband. Not being a Christian man, he had not known who to blame, except her. But they had one more trip to the big house for Christmas. Edward, forced on by the memory of his parents, tried as hard as he could to pull any memory of the house from his head. He vaguely recalled a sparkling Christmas tree, and pulling a cracker with a freckle-faced girl, but his mother's death in January had blackened his memory of her then to dust and there seemed nothing left to rescue. xxx

Edward woke, physically drained.

***

Yulia felt grateful, almost saying thanks to God, whom she had disowned, when Kirill finally left her alone and went back to his Suite.

She wished she could give him her body to stop him shouting, but he didn't want her, and of course there was Yuri.

The drive to the station and the train ride had been full of what she called 'man talk,' leaving her blissfully free to consider her day. The jet engine demonstration had been an inspired idea. She thought of it in the morning, because she missed Edward already, though she did not want to admit it. She told Kirill the visit might allow her to find out more about the engine and trap Edward more firmly in her web. Kirill believed her.

Yulia loved the mad screaming of the jet engine, the odour of oil, gasoline and burnt air, a kind of alchemy that intoxicated her. Others sometimes called it witchcraft, but to her the engines sounded just like Angels singing, or screaming, an unearthly song.

Most of all she loved the look on Edward's face; his petulant anger at her intrusion. In that moment, she knew she had him, but in the same moment, *he* had *her*. She had fallen for him completely and there could be no doubt left in her mind.

On the train, she went over all the half-truths she had told him about her childhood and wondered which of the lies he might have detected.

"He seems a clever man," she told herself, "but perhaps a little naïve. Perhaps he won't spot any. I do hope so. If he doesn't believe enough of it, he won't love me."

Her instructor, The Bitch, as she came to call the woman, had told her another surprising fact; that few men love a woman whose vulnerability they cannot see, and the easiest way to show this is to talk about your childhood – make it up if necessary. Of course, this had presented Yulia with a few problems, but her half-truths seemed to have worked.

***

Once Yulia had heard she had been assigned to the NKVD mission to Derby, her life's course took a very different turn. Her uncle in the Service told her to expect a letter and to follow its instructions explicitly, but to tell Yuri nothing.

The letter had arrived with a return ticket to Istanbul, a street address and a brief note, which told her to learn as much Turkish as she could, not to miss the flight and make sure she reached the address without being followed.

It had taken Yulia nearly four hours to find the large townhouse, two bus rides from Istanbul airport, and the delay did not impress the matron. She screwed up her face, one so flat that it seemed she had run into a wall, but gently pushed back a stray strand of brown hair over her left ear, giving Yulia the misguided notion that the woman couldn't be all bad.

"Why are you late comrade?" the woman hissed, in a large room with brown walls.

"I cannot speak Turkish fluently yet, so had to ask many people for directions."

"Well, you will have to show more initiative *here*! You know what we do?"

"No."

"We train girls, pretty girls like you, to extract information from foreigners. You will use your intelligence, charm, beauty, and if required, your body, to get this information."

Yulia saw the slightest trace of a smirk pass over the woman's garishly red lips and couldn't decide if this indicated pleasure at shocking Yulia, or at the weakness of men. But Yulia's calm curiosity quickly wiped the smirk from the older woman's face, so she continued:

"I can see you are a clever and beautiful young woman. I don't think you will have much trouble getting the information. Provided that you are motivated."

This hidden warning made Yulia suddenly straighten her back and reply:

"I am loyal to the State Colonel."

Yulia, like most Russians, hated Germans after they invaded Russia, so she felt pleased when her first assignment turned out to be a Luftwaffe pilot. Posing as Ludmilla, a Turkish prostitute, she picked him up in a bar and took him back to her room, which looked a little more squalid that she would have liked, in a cheap hotel rented for the purpose by the NKVD.

Her main difficulty proved to be resisting the urge to tell him she was Russian and couldn't under-stand what he said. She knew enough German to do business, but her cover story required her to pose as an Armenian. She added an embellishment of her own, that she had a sick daughter, who needed special healthcare.

Germany had ceased selling aircraft to Turkey almost a year before, but some wounded pilots were still sent there to train the country's own novice pilots. Hans had sustained a wound in the lower abdomen, which made walking difficult and rendered him, to all intents and purposes, impotent. Yulia's unswerving attention therefore flattered him, and the dull shadow of depression in his eyes seemed to lift when she let him remove her clothes. She felt no shame about her birthmark with such men, indeed, she had discovered that it made her more attractive to them.

"You know, until now, I never thought life could be worth living again Ludmilla," he murmured. "But I have never seen a woman as beautiful as you and I never dreamed I would see one *naked*. Just to touch and kiss you is a bliss I hadn't imagined."

Yulia cooed and coaxed, so that before long he would talk about nothing else, but the state of the Luftwaffe and the collapse of Germany:

"Hitler tells us we will still win, that we have the V1 and the V2 and even a V3 – not that anybody seems to know what this *is* – but it's all pipe-dreams! We pilots know the score. There are few enough of us left to fly the planes we *do* have. And there is no fuel to put in them. We may as well sell *all of them* to Turkey, although the buyer would have to collect!"

At times like these, Yulia often pretended to sleep, but diligently memorised any fact or rumour he repeated to her serene face. She felt a momentary pang of pity for Hans, but felt much better when she wiped it from her heart and told herself how easily she could now seduce and exploit any man. Her first mission had been a success, but now, of course, she had found Edward.

***

Yulia leaned over the washbasin, holding a sharp knife blade against her wrist. Few, but her, would have noticed the thin, livid scar on her wrist, which she used now as a guide for the second cut. She stared at her reflection in the mirror, grotesquely blurred by a torrent of tears.

She hated herself most for asking Edward about Don. Her life had become a misery of lies and deception. In the Soviet Union, everyone encouraged deception, as if it were a virtue, and she alone seemed to have a memory of anything different. All men seemed distant, echoes of her father in Porozhek, although she thought she remembered something better from her early years. She wanted to believe in a world of honest, caring people, but it had finally become impossible. Even if Edward did feel something like love for her, she would bring about his certain death. She could see it now, the only thing she could see clearly in the black room of her innermost thoughts. Her aching heart told her to slice her wrists and end it all, but another emotion, at first, feeble, began to emerge from the darkness.

Most would probably think that a beautiful woman would be conscious of her beauty at all times, but that wasn't the case with Yulia. Her beauty had developed well after her character had been beaten out by circumstance, so she wore it much as one might wear a coat. She could take it off at any time, and such a time had come. Now she confronted her deepest feelings and found that she wanted to care for somebody. She wanted to love somebody, and so she would try to live. But she felt dizzy and still had to make sense of things.

Kirill had told her earlier that day:

"Torrens went back to the car when we reached the factory. I think he kept the shavings from the car. He *definitely* knows and he wants proof! He is going to talk! The bastard is definitely going to talk, but to whom? The British M.I.6 are watching him closely and we believe they have talked to him, but he hasn't told them yet. We would know. So at least you have done *that* part well. He *has* fallen for you, but he has to tell somebody. Find out who his friends are, who he trusts."

Kirill knew about Don, so the man would be marked. They would probably try to blackmail him, but she hadn't wanted to worry about that. She didn't have a clear plan, and defection was out, for now, but she knew she had to keep both herself and Edward alive. Somehow.

The show in London had started the evening well. It had brought back distant memories of childhood. Stanley Hooker had insisted on sitting next to her in the theatre, so she found herself sandwiched between Hooker and Mikoyan, which didn't please Kirill.

'I am going to pay for this later,' she told herself.

When she left the auditorium for the ladies' room, Gregori tapped Kirill's shoulder, and the dour commander man nodded. Gregori followed Yulia and stole a violent kiss in the darkness.

"Not here you idiot!" Yulia protested. "It is too dangerous."

Kirill barely waited until they had reached her Suite before he tossed off his coat, usually a sign of trouble, and began berating her:

"Why are you so friendly with Hooker now? Are you trying to ally with him? I don't trust you and this Torrens. You are both up to something!"

"Kirill! Please! You *can* trust me! I am doing my best!"

"You are a lying bitch! You have always been difficult. Everyone knows it. And on the train Mikoyan told me how unhappy he is with security aspects of this operation. We will all be demoted if this goes wrong! And I don't intend for my career to be fucked up by a stupid little blonde whore, who is barely more than a child. Now tell me what is going on?"

Kirill Bregovsky grabbed Yulia's wrists and shook her, making the chain pendant smash into her teeth. She resisted, so he pushed her over the arm of a chair, sending her sprawling. Her head hit the floor, making her dizzy. She shook herself and tried to stand, but he fell upon her again. This time he grabbed a fistful of her hair and shook her, growling:

"Take off that dress. I would rip it off, but it's worth more than you!"

She shook her head, gasping, determined not to cry.

"Do it!" he bellowed.

"But Yuri? You promised him!"

"I don't care!" he bellowed.

"You will wake the whole Hotel! Do you want them throwing us out?"

"They won't do that. Do it!"

More than the humiliation being inflicted on her by Kirill and the danger of Yuri finding out, she wanted to avoid Edward's pity and embarrassment. Fearing sure that Edward could hear the commotion, she reluctantly complied, removing the jewellery first and then submitting to Kirill's clumsy hands on the buttons on the dress. When she stepped free of the white cotton sheath, she wore only her underwear.

'Perhaps he will do it to me and then this will be finished,' she hoped.

But Kirill slowly unfastened his leather belt, fixing a hungry look on her that made tears well in her eyes.

"No, Kirill!"

She squeezed her eyes shut to stop the tears, but they came nevertheless, as if too simple a physical reaction for her to control. He approached her, hissing:

"You have one last chance. Tell me what you have agreed with him?"

"Nothing! I tell you, nothing!"

"I will teach you not to betray us. Bend over that table."

"You can't do this!" she sobbed. "If you damage me, he won't want me. *You* will be fired, not me!"

Kirill let out a feral growl, which became a howl, before he formed the word, "Bitch!" in the back of his throat. He stormed out of the room, leaving the door open.

Now Yulia considered Kirill Bregovsky in a cold light. She knew how important he was to the delegation's plans and how important he could be to *her* plans. She considered Kirill a clever man, but also a predicable one, so perhaps she could exploit that. The thought cheered her.

Doors began to close in her mind, like the beat of footsteps, which came ever closer, accompanied by the shrill whistle of a train, until she heard a 'Bang!'

"Yulia? It's Kirill. Are you awake?"

Yulia nearly jumped out of her skin, but fought her Soviet conditioning with all her might. Putting down her knife, she gripped the edge of the washbasin so hard that her knuckles turned white. Yulia knew that a Russian woman should never ignore a man, but she did. She held on. The loud knocks came on the door again and the deep voice, whispering:

"Yulia? Are you awake?"

It was Kirill. She held on to the basin until the feeling to resist began to waver. Just about to give in and answer, she suddenly heard footsteps recede from the other side of the door. Shaking, she let go of the basin and wiped the tears from her cheeks. She washed her face without looking at her reflection in the mirror.

When she turned toward the bedroom, she decided that her bed looked like the rack of old Ivan the Terrible stories. She laid herself upon it, but only out of habit; sleep didn't want her. Still wearing only her underwear, she stole out of the Suite and padded to Edward's door. Pressing her body against the door, she kissed it, leaving a lipstick rosette.

***

Edward rose on Wednesday and left without turning to look at the door. A cleaner later wiped away the lipstick kiss.

Dreading work, but finding his thoughts much clearer, Edward exchanged a few knowing glances with Don. He felt relieved that nothing unexpected happened, until he received a memo in the 11.30 post: 'Be in my office at 2.30. Sanderson.'

Fearing the worst again, he instead found Sanderson with Kirill Mikoyan and Yulia, who wore a primrose summer dress. She looked tired, her expression so stony that not even her cheek muscles quivered when he entered.

"Ah Edward!" Sanderson began. "Mister Mikoyan and Mister Bregovsky want to talk to me about some aspects of the ... arrangement and we were wondering if you would like to take Miss Panedolia into Derby for the afternoon?"

"But ... ."

"It's alright!" Sanderson retorted, raising his hand. "The blueprints and packing are well underway and we could think of nobody better to show her around. I'm sure Miss Panedolia will be delighted to sample English town life."

Sanderson's knitted eyebrows left no room for manoeuvre, so Edward acquiesced with a nod.

"Good," Sanderson replied. "The limousine is at the entrance. We won't need it today. Have fun!"

Edward led Yulia out of the office by her elbow and whispered:

"He must have enjoyed that last gesture of generosity. The man is a selfish bastard most of the time. And tight as a … . Well, never mind."

"You're not angry with me?"

"I've learned that anger is pointless with you."

"Good. Let's go."

"So what do you want to see first?" he asked, helping her onto the back seat of the Daimler.

"Oh, I don't care. We can just drive around."

He thought she wore more powder on her cheeks than usual.

"You look tired," he said.

"Yes … ."

"Look, I … ."

"Don't say it. I would bet you heard something last night. Let's just enjoy today. Please?"

"Alright. Just shopping then. I used to shop with Ewa … ."

"Oh, who is she? An old girlfriend? You didn't tell me … ?"

"She was my fiancée. But she was killed by a V2 bomb during the War."

"Oh."

"It's alright. I wanted you to know."

Pleased with his confession, Yulia held his hand as he rested it on his leg. She watched the shops as they flickered past the car window, frame by frame, but it wasn't a movie that absorbed her.

Edward's hand twitched involuntarily, so she turned to face him. Staring into her big, brown eyes made him lose his chain of thought completely.

"So what shops can we look at?" Yulia asked.

"Oh. Well, apart from a few restaurants, haberdashers, tea houses and Woolworths, I doubt there is much in Derby to interest a Russian beauty!"

"What is Woolworths?" Yulia pronounced the name carefully.

"Ha! It's a shop that has everything; clothes, toys, records ... . I used to spend hours there as a kid. Every town has one."

"Let's go there then!"

Yulia's face lit up, making Edward laugh.

"Drop us off at Woolworths," Edward told the chauffeur. "And come back in ... what ... ?" He looked at Yulia.

She mouthed, "Three hours."

"Three hours please!"

The car stopped a few yards from the shop, so Edward led Yulia in. Her eyes widened at the sight of so many bright, shiny things:

"Wow! We have nothing like this in Russia, except maybe in Moscva."

Edward led Yulia, in a haphazard way, toward the boys' toys area. She let her fingers brush against every packet and trinket within reach, but by the time he stopped, she had turned into another aisle and picked up a pink, plastic bead necklace.

"How much is this?" she asked.

"Oh Yulia!" Edward had to check the display before he could tell her the price:

"Sixpence! It's just a toy; barely more than a Christmas cracker toy!"

Yulia gave Edward a long, penetrating look and replied:

"I want it. May I have it?"

"Do you have English money?"

"Don't tease me. You are my chaperone for the day. Can you afford it?"

"Oh I think so."

Edward paid for the necklace and they moved on.

"That was a mistake," Yulia said to him.

With a determined pucker to her mouth, she sought other girlish trinkets to take back to Russia. She began with a pair of pink earrings and fairy-wings, both which Edward paid for. Then she spotted the records.

"What is good?" she asked.

"What do you like?"

"Jazz. Big bands – swing."

"Alright. I don't know much about jazz, but I know Duke Ellington is good," he told her, holding up the brightly coloured cover.

Next to the plain brown, English sleeves, it looked gaudy, so Yulia grabbed it, exclaiming:

"Oh yes! I *like* the Duke. I will take that back with me! What else?"

She spent some time picking five records before taking one last look around the shop. Stretching her neck and standing on tiptoes, she reminded Edward of a desert mammal he had seen in a book.

"You make me laugh!" he told her.

But Yulia had seen something, so set off. Edward had to weave recklessly through the aisles to keep up with her. She grabbed a miniature white dress and held it up to cover her, asking him:

"Does it suit me?"

"Well, it only reaches your waist, so I think you would look indecent if you wore it."

"Oh." Her mock crestfallen expression reminded him that she could pretend very well, but he shook his head to clear the thought.

"How about this?" he asked, holding up a miniature BOAC stewardess cap.

"Oh yes. I love that! But will it fit?"

She balanced the tiny cap on her head, but Edward watched it start to slide off. Catching it, he handed it to her. She threw it at him, declaring:

"If I can't wear it, I will give it to someone. I think I'm finished."

"How about this?" Edward asked, holding up a red pinafore, which wasn't much shorter than Yulia's dress.

"Not my colour. I never wear red, except lipstick. Come on."

She brushed past him and he couldn't be sure if the energy that made his skin tingle was static electricity, or something else.

"That will be four pounds and seventeen shillings sir," said the cashier.

Edward took out his wallet and extracted a five-pound note while Yulia's cast an inquisitive glance inside his wallet.

"Now where," she asked, adding, "What was it you told me; tea houses? Don't they have them in China?"

"We have them here too, but different. You have to try scones though."

"What are scones?"

"You'll see."

Yulia casually looped her arm around Edward's, whose hand had been stuck in his pocket in that way that English men did when they were strolling. He led her past many shops, none of which caught her eye for more than an instant. The sun beat its late summer rays down upon their cheeks, making Edward wonder why he had never been so happy during any other summer.

"I can hardly believe the sun is so strong. We are always told England is dark and wet!" Yulia ventured.

"It usually is. Here we go!"

He found a small café and after checking that it served tea cakes and scones, led Yulia to a wrought iron table, overlooking the street.

The waitress came and took Edward's order of a pot of tea for two and a round of scones with jam and cream.

"This is going to be expensive," Edward observed. Yulia's knitted brows demanded an explanation. "Rationing. Cream and jam are still scarce."

Within a minute another waitress placed the pot of tea on the table.

Edward swilled the hot liquid around in the tea pot and poured an experimental cup. It came out paler than he would have liked, but he felt thirsty, so he added a dash of milk and tried the tea, declaring:

"Not bad. A bit bitter."

Slanting sun rays cast the right side of Yulia's beautiful face into the shadow of her hair, bewitching him, so that he couldn't speak.

"What are you looking at Edward?"

"Your face. You're so beautiful."

"Thank you. You know, it's actually too hot. If I could, I would take something off."

Edward almost choked on his mouthful of tea. The scones arrived.

"Try one," Edward suggested.

"Aren't you going to have one?"

"Of course. I just wanted to see what you thought."

"What do I do?"

Edward felt the heat radiating from the windows and saw that the thin wedge of yellow butter had already started to melt.

"Cut the scone in two and butter it. Then add as much jam and cream as you like."

Yulia followed his instructions and took a bite.

"Um. Delicious. We have something like it in Russia, but not so sweet."

Edward prepared a scone to his own taste. Yulia watched what he did.

"Where's your Woolworths bag," he asked, suddenly remembering that he hadn't seen her bring it in to the shop.

"Right here. By my feet. It's safe."

As if she thought he made too light of her life, she suddenly seemed to veer toward seriousness by asking:

"Tell me about Ewa?"

"Oh, not much to say. Enjoyed dancing together and the 'done thing' was to marry. So, we became engaged. I mean; the War made us feel the end was always near. Everything seemed to be so urgent. Oh, it doesn't matter."

"And your wife? Viktoria?"

"We haven't … ."

"Haven't what?"

"Nothing. English people don't talk about such things. It's not done."

"You haven't made love?"

"Well, yes … . I suppose so. Haven't even slept together. Not for a long time."

Edward immediately regretted revealing such intimate details, feeling that somehow he had betrayed Viktoria.

"She doesn't want to? Won't?"

"Oh, can we change the subject? We just weren't right for each other and we didn't learn that until too late. It makes it harder to deal with when it was inevitable from the start."

"You feel guilty, you mean."

Edward gave Yulia a cold glare, so she looked away.

"I'm sorry Edward for being so rude. I was just curious. What are you going to do?"

"Do?"

"Look!" she nodded in the direction of the window. "There's nobody listening. Kirill tells me the British Secret Service is watching you, but they are not now. Did you know they were watching you?"

"No," he lied.

"Artyom saw you go back to the car. He knows you took the filings from the floor," she countered. "Did you do it to protect me?"

"No. Yes. Initially, yes. But then … ."

"What?"

But Edward already felt he had said too much.

Yulia leaned forward and put her hand on his knuckle, whispering:

"Do you think we are worth a chance?"

Edward looked into her eyes. He longer for her, but he could say nothing.

"Nobody is here. Look around you. This may be the only chance we get to talk openly."

"The Hotel?"

"I don't know. Kirill is getting suspicious. Stop fooling yourself Edward. We don't have much time left."

"Do you … feel the same way about me that I feel about you?"

"I think so."

Her hand remained warm to touch. Edward remembered that his mother had told him, "Warm hands, warm heart," and he believed her, despite the usual adage saying the opposite. His mind swung into top gear:

"I can't let them win Yulia; Kirill and Mikoyan. I have to stop them."

"I know that."

"But I also want to save you. Could you defect?"

"Ha! Save a drowning witch! Yes, I read your history, how your country treated witches." She shook her head. "I don't think so. They will be watching me. They would kill me first. And anyway, I couldn't leave Yuri."

"You love him?"

Yulia thought for a long time before replying.

"No. But he helped me so much. Without him … . No, I couldn't do it."

Edward nodded, but the tortured look she gave him, combined with a sharp pain in his own gut, almost made him choke again.

"I kept the shavings," he said. "I hid them. I don't know what to do with them though."

"I will help you. So, are we together?"

"Yes. You know it," he replied.

"Good."

She squeezed his hand.

"I hope I can trust you," he added. "Can you get the shavings back? The ones you took?"

"I don't think so. We have to be very careful. They have other agents here. They will kill me, or you, if they think it will help them. You should throw away the shavings."

"I can't do that. It's the only proof I have."

"But it implicates you. Why else would you have picked them up?"

"Yes. You're right. I can't see the solution."

"Do you love me?"

"Yes."

For a long time, they stared into each other's eyes, hands clasped on the wrought-iron table.

"And the shavings?" he asked.

"It doesn't matter now. Can we go to a little park? I would like to see some flowers and trees."

"Yes, I'm sure there will be one near here. I'll ask."

When he returned from the counter Yulia had lit a cigarette.

"Do you have a matchbox?" he asked.

"Why?"

"Don't ask questions. Trust me."

"Somewhere in my bag. I'll find it."

They left the café and headed for the small park that the waitress had told him about, a triangle of grass within rows of flowers and a path. At the centre stood some old oak and beech trees.

As they circulated on the gravel path the shade from the tall trees cooled them. A gentle breeze played with the topmost sprigs and wafted Yulia's golden tresses.

"Will we have lots of children?" Yulia asked.

"But we can't Yulia! We're both married!"

"Yes, but just imagine! Just dream for a moment! What if we weren't?"

"Then three boys and a girl!"

"No. Three girls and a boy!"

"Ha. Maybe two of each then."

"And where will we live?"

"In a big house in Dorking. Where my father still lives."

"Oh? They are separated?"

"No. My mother died."

"Oh. Sorry."

"It was a long time ago."

They walked on, hand in hand, for six more turns without speaking a word. The sun hung lower in the dome of blue, encouraging the breeze to play more vigorously with Yulia's hair. Edward swung her into his arms and kissed her ruby-red lips.

"What was that for?" she asked, giggling.

"Because you are so beautiful and I will miss you, this evening, if we aren't together."

"Oh, we will be. I will make sure of *that*! Kirill is my boss, but he is not my master."

"Hm. A subtle distinction."

"Edward?" Yulia suddenly looked very serious.

"Yes?"

"Even if things don't work out here – I mean *if* I am still alive – I will wait in Russia until things have changed and then perhaps I will come to you. For a visit. Will you wait for me?"

"Yes."

"Even ten years?"

"Of course."

For the first time, Edward imagined not being married to Viktoria in ten years' time, but the thought quickly left his mind.

An up-current lifted a few strands of hair over Yulia's ear, allowing a beam of sunlight to spark into Edward's eye.

"Did I tell you that your eyes remind me of the sky near Leningrad?" Yulia whispered.

"No!" Edward yelled. He gripped her by the waist and spun her round him like a child's fairground swing. Yulia squealed with delight.

"Put me down Edward! Why are you doing this?"

"I'm so happy!"

"We should go back," she said, when he put her down. "Kirill will start asking questions."

"Yes. Oh Lord! I forgot the limousine!" He checked his watch. "Ten minutes. That's lucky! Come on!"

He led her in a race to Woolworths, where they found the limousine still waiting.

***

The factory had closed, so they asked the chauffeur to take them straight to the Midland Hotel.

Edward went to his Suite, took a bath and ordered a meal from room service. He listened for voices in Yulia's Suite, but everything seemed very quiet. After eating, he began to plan what he would do. The quickest way to find The Vapour seemed to be to walk into town. He already had the cigarette packet, but the problem seemed to be how to get out of the Hotel without the Russians noticing. If he saw him, they would have him followed. He couldn't think of a solution on his own and the bar seemed the best option for a chance to meet his accomplice, so he dressed and went downstairs.

Two beers later, he had just begun to think he should head for town when two police officers walked in with Stanley Hooker. They walked straight up to Edward and Hooker said:

"Edward. There's been an accident. You need to come with us right away."

Hooker looked scared. The police officers led them to a blue and white squad car and a third police man drove them toward the factory.

"What's going on?" Edward asked Hooker.

"Wait. You will find out soon enough."

At the factory two of the officers led the way to Hooker's office and one of them closed the door. Edward glimpsed two figures in white coats move in tandem past the rippled glass window in the door.

"Sit down Edward," Hooker said, standing awkwardly against his own table. "I'm sorry to drag you into this, but you were the only person I could think of who could help."

Edward, who had just perched nervously on the edge of the leather chair, relaxed and reclined.

"There has been a death," began the taller of the two officers. "A Mister Donald Hill."

An ice-cold chill ran down Edward's spine. He knew he must have turned as white as a sheet, but gathered his nerve enough to ask:

"What happened?"

The tall officer turned to Hooker, who coughed and began, uncertainly:

"It seems Mister Hill – I didn't know him personally, but I understand you were good friends with him Edward, so this is going to be hard – he stayed late to dissemble parts on the Nene engine on Test Bed 2. There was nobody else around when he started up the engine ... ."

Edward looked up and stared at Hooker with a look that pleaded for an explanation. Hooker continued:

"He must have disabled the master lock, because he managed to start the engine while *inside* the chamber itself. Then he ... well ... he stuck his head inside the intake. I needn't tell you the rest. It will take a few days to clear up the mess. Nobody's to go near it until then."

Hooker levered himself up from the desk and paced the room:

"It's all taped off anyway. At the moment, we're treating it as an accident, but ... it looks more like suicide. At least, you have to admit, with the master lock tampered with ... . That's what the Detective Inspector says."

Hooker nodded back to the tall officer, who took up the story:

"Yes. Thank you Mister Hooker. We believe there is a chance it's suicide, but we understand that a very sensitive transaction between us and the Russians is underway at the moment. We certainly wouldn't be able to even suggest suicide as a possible cause for a few days, at least until late Saturday."

The officer fell silent and Edward guessed that they expected him to speak, but he found that he had to clear his throat before he could force any words out:

"Yes, I see. Very sensitive."

Inside Edward, voices clamoured for attention, telling him that:

"Don must have been murdered by the Russians. They must have been seen together and the Russians assumed he told them something."

Another voice, as cold as a judge, retorted:

"But why didn't they kill *me*?"

Edward tried to force the voices to be quiet and smiled weakly at the officer, praying that the policeman wasn't perceptive enough to see anything in his eyes.

"Anyway," the officer said, suddenly seeming to come to a decision and folding his arms, "We would like to ask you a few questions to help us get a feel for the man."

"Fine."

"Did he talk to you about his debts?"

"Debts? No. I didn't know he had any!"

"Some were gambling debts. But I don't think they were significant. At least they were brought about by his greater debt; a mortgage he had fallen so far behind with that the house was due to be repossessed."

"I knew nothing about it."

"What sort of man was he? Hard working? Honest? Would he have been vulnerable to, say, bribes?"

"Don? I don't think so. He was a family man, steady as a rock. Good sportsman and as honest a Yorkshireman as you'll ever find."

"You trusted him?"

"Yes."

The Detective Inspector scratched his chin and thought of another question:

"The master lock. How does it work?"

"Well, it's very simple. Underneath a cover is a small lever. If it's at the vertical position, a contact is made and the engine cannot be started while the door is open. That's it."

"So it could be easily disabled?"

"Yes. But Don would never do that, normally. There are warning stickers all over it. It's painted red. These things are not messed with by engineers of Don's calibre."

Edward didn't say what he thought:

'Don must have disabled the switch. Don must have killed himself. The Russians must have made him do it! They *must* want me too!' His thoughts spun faster and faster, like runaway turbine blades.

"Unless he *wanted* to kill himself," The officer added.

"Yes."

"One last question if you don't mind. Please think hard before answering. Take your time. Is there anything, anything at all, that you noticed, or Don said to you, in the last few days, which might make you think, on reflection, that he wanted to end it all?"

Edward counted to sixty before answering:

"No. I honestly can't think of anything."

"Hmph! Very well, I think that's all. Don't' stray too far from Derby until Saturday Mister Torrens. We may want to ask you more questions."

Edward couldn't wait to get away, but as the officers left, Hooker pulled him aside:

"Edward. Not a word of this to anybody. We're comforting the family – Mrs Hill – now. If you know her, stay away. This will be a very stressful time for them."

It sounded like a warning, but Edward had no intention of visiting Delores.

"How do I get back to the Hotel sir?"

"I'll drive you. Wait while I get my hat and coat. I seem to have left them somewhere."

***

Back at the Midland Hotel, Edward felt he needed a stiff drink. He half-hoped to see Yulia, but couldn't find her in the restaurant, or bar. After two scotches, he had worked up the courage to seek out The Vapour, but his fingers still trembled when he turned the handle on the Hotel front door and stepped into the cool air. The Vapour found *him* shortly after he dropped the crumpled cigarette packet into a gutter on Victoria Street.

"I've been wanting a little chat with you," the husky voice told him, between puffs on yet another cigarette. The agent had a trilby hat pulled low over his brow, so that his eyes were completely obliterated by shadow.

"Why?"

"Our friend Don. Bit of a shock, isn't it?"

"Yes. He was my friend."

"Yes, and now he's dead. You were both seen together, in his car, yesterday."

"Yes. So?"

"We believe it wasn't suicide. We believe the Russians are up to something. One of their agents was seen chatting to Don in a pub the night before last. Of course, Don wouldn't have *known* he was an agent. He would have seemed just like any other drunk local. Did you know he had big debts?"

"No. The police just asked me the same question."

"Oh, them. We told them to go easy on you. But I have my suspicions."

They were shuffling along, side by side, but now Edward had to make a choice, cross a street or turn a corner. He turned into a side street.

"What do you mean?"

"What did you and Don chat about? The Russians?"

"No ... . We talked about the move of our teams to Derby."

"And you told Don that if he didn't help you and the Russians steal engine parts, you would tell Delores about the debts?"

Edward stopped in his tracks and faced the shadow under the hat.

"No! Hold on! Wait a minute! You're pointing the finger at *me*!"

"That's the way it's looking right now Mister Torrens."

"Look, I would never do that to a friend! And I am *not* involved with the Russians! Quite the opposite in fact ... ." He almost told The Vapour about the shavings.

"We've been watching you closely Torrens. We know about Yulia. We think you're up to something. One more slip from you and you're out!"

The shadow turned, stepped off the pavement and merged into the night.

Edward shouted, "I never asked to be *in*!" but he felt that he had already been dropped from the scaffold. He stood still, breathing hard, for a long while, before he gathered his nerve to walk back to the Hotel. He felt a combination of anger and cold fear, a mixture he had never experienced before. Way out of his depth, he felt

that the Derby streets were wreathed in a cold fog, a
shade that he couldn't see, but only feel.

***

He found Yulia in the bar.

"Thank god you came!" she said. "I only
managed to get away for ten minutes. I heard about what
happened! It's terrible. I worried about you. Did they
accuse you?"

"No," Edward replied, holding her fluttering
hands at arm's length. "It must be your side! It *must* be!
The only mystery is why they killed *him* and not *me*!"

"Keep your voice down!" she whispered.

The barman polished a glass studiously, but
Edward guessed the Latino had heard something, so he
led Yulia to a table.

"Did you know this would happen?" Edward
hissed.

"No! Honestly. No!"

Edward stared into her brown eyes for a long
time before he felt sure she told the truth.

"They suspect *me*!" he gasped.

"What? Why?"

"I don't know!"

He gripped her elbow and kissed her. Her lips
wore no makeup and he could smell the faintly sweet,
natural odour of her body for the first time. He kissed
her again, whispering:

"Go back to your Suite. I will think of
something. Don't worry. I love you!"

Yulia kissed him back and left.

"There was a call for you sir," the barman said,
after catching Edward's eye. "I didn't want to say
anything until now. From your wife. She sounded very
worried, if I might say so."

The barman's face remained the picture of indifference.

"Of course," Edward replied, blushing. "Thanks. I'll call her from my suite."

On his way past reception Edward gave the concierge his home number and then hurried to his Suite, where he found the telephone already ringing.

"Hello dear," he said. "How are you?"

"Oh Edward! Delores called me. She's distraught! I'm worried about you too? What is going on?"

Edward felt relieved for an instant, then guiltier than he had ever felt in his life, and had to swallow before he could find the words to reply with:

"Yes, Don's gone. It's terrible. They've been asking me questions. Things haven't been going well dear."

"Oh, you poor thing. I'll come down straight away!"

"No dear! No!" Edward replied quickly. "Don't do that. The whole thing is top secret!"

"But I'm bored anyway. And now I'm worried!"

Edward had never expected this turn of events. Viktoria hadn't shown him any warmth for a long time and to have her suddenly worrying about him made everything so much more complicated.

"Don't worry dear! I will call you tomorrow. I … I have to go. Take care. Bye!"

"Do you have a bottle of vodka?" he asked the barman.

"Certainly sir. Here you are."

"How much?"

"It will be on the Rolls bill sir."

"Thanks. And a glass."

Edward poured himself a glass of vodka and lay on his bed, thinking hard. He had to open the window against the oppressive heat, but still started to sweat, so undressed to his vest and underpants.

"How have I got into this mess? It's ridiculous! And yet I can't back out now! I have to think!"

But think as he might, he could not come up with a solution and underneath his own fear and confusion lay his pain for the loss of Don. Guilt complicated his grief and only after a long while did he fall into a fitful sleep.

Chapter Four

Sing a song of sixpence,
A pocket full of rye.
Four and twenty blackbirds,
Baked in a pie.

When the pie was opened,
The birds began to sing;
Wasn't that a dainty dish,
To set before the king?

The king was in his counting house,
Counting out his money;
The queen was in the parlour,
Eating bread and honey.

The maid was in the garden,
Hanging out the clothes,
When down came a blackbird
And pecked off her nose.

A girl's singing woke Edward. Though he still wore his vest and underpants, a cold draft from the open window made goose pimples on his arm. The rhyme made him smile, but then memories of the previous night crashed in. He threw his arm over his eyes and groaned.

"What have I done?"

He dressed automatically and ate breakfast in the dining room, seeking protection of the crowd from any more awkward questions. With his heart weighed down by despair, he thought of calling his father.

'But he can't help me. It would only drag him into something.'

Another thought chipped away at his consciousness until he had to examine it. Something that had surprised him shortly after he arrived on the Sunday came into focus; a call that had come through to his Suite:

"Hello?"

"Edward? Is that you? It's your old man."

"Dad? How the hell did you get my number? How did you even *know* I was *here*?"

Edward never spoke to his father unless strictly necessary and hadn't told him about the Russian delegation. He hadn't even told Sam, yet somehow his father knew. It didn't make sense.

"I just wanted to check you arrived safely. Is everything alright?"

"Yes … . I guess so. But how did you know dad?"

"Oh, I have my contacts. Anyway. Perhaps we can talk later in the week. I would love a visit from you, since you are a bit further down south for a change."

"Okay dad. I will try if I get time, but things are pretty hectic right now. Take care of yourself."

"Oh. Alright. Good bye."

"Bye."

Edward had tried to puzzle out how his father could possibly have known about the delegation, but failed to find an answer and dismissed the incident. Now he puzzled over it again. Did his father know Hooker? The idea had occurred before. His rise through the ranks *had* seemed rapid, so Perhaps Hooker was a drinker and knew his father through that. Edward dismissed the thought again when the Daimler reached the factory.

Only two Rolls executives accompanied him when he stepped out of the car. Edward still couldn't understand why the Russians had killed Don and not him, because Don knew nothing, except the location of the shavings. With no meeting until 10 am, Edward had plenty of time to check his drawer. The shavings were still in the spare spectacles case, wrapped in the handkerchief.

Edward tried to be tidy in his professional life, some might even have thought him fastidious, but his desk drawer had become his refuge. It contained every manner of knick-knack, from a green, Hornby railway crane, which somebody had long ago given him to repair, to a pencil sharpener with an eraser jammed inside. On the right side of the drawer, however, sat a neat pile of notebooks. He had written notes in a large, black one, only the day before. It sat at the top then, but now it lay third from the top. Somebody had been through his desk.

'But cleaners are not allowed to open drawers,' he recalled. 'Not legitimate ones anyway. And it couldn't have been the Russians; they could never get in here. The cleaners all have security clearance. It has to be M.I.6! Thank god the shaving are still here, but *now* I have to move them. Idiots!'

Edward thanked his lucky stars that M.I.6 and the Russians didn't talk to each other, for if they had, his shavings would have been gone and he probably would be heading for the gallows. Now he had to hide them.

"But have they been tampered with?"

He took out the spectacles case and inspected the shavings. One of them still had its distinctive, curled end, so he wrapped them up again and put the handkerchief in his inside, breast pocket.

'Don can't have told the Russians anything, *if* they *did* force him to take his own life.'

The beginnings of a theory grew in Edward's mind:

'If they knew we talked and believed Don had nothing to lose by going to the authorities, perhaps that would be enough to tip the scales. After the Russian agent got wind of his debts – it was true Don could be talkative when drunk, but Edward hadn't wanted to tell the Police this – perhaps somebody telephoned Don and gave him a stark choice. But they couldn't know he would *top* himself! Unless … they pretended to be M.I.6 and told him they had something on him about working with the Russians.'

"Oh Don! Surely you couldn't have been such a fool! But I'm to blame! I told you just enough to implicate you, but not enough to give you anything to bargain with!"

Edward had to supervise the loading of ten engines and completion of the blueprints. His Nene team worked in a morbid daze. Nobody wanted to talk about Don, but they didn't want to talk about anything else, so nobody spoke. At lunchtime, a call came through to Edward from Viktoria:

"Hello. Viktoria?"

"You said you'd call me!" Her voice sounded shrill.

"Sorry! We've been so busy!"

"Anyway, I've been with Delores all morning. She's in a terrible state. And the kids! Well anyway, she told me Don mentioned some Russian woman you're seeing. Is it true Edward? I want to know!"

"What's it to you? How about your affair? I hardly think you have a righ- … ."

"Maybe I don't, but this whole thing is really fishy. I'm coming down as soon as I can, maybe today, but I don't know if I can leave Delores now. If not, then tomorrow. I booked a room in the Hotel. They can't stop me *paying for my own room!*"

Viktoria's voice had risen to such a crescendo that Edward barely understood the last few words. After the call ended he stood still for a while, listening to the ringing in his ears, but then dismissed her arrival as yet another thing beyond his control.

***

voila

Yulia had been able to spend some time on her own that afternoon. After a meeting with Bregovsky, Mikoyan and Klimov, she lay down to rest on her bed and found her thoughts wandering to her first and only holiday with Yuri. He came to her flat one night in an excited mood:

"Have you heard? They are giving out free passes to the newly captured holiday resorts on the Black Sea. We can go!"

"But Yuri. We don't need free passes! We're not poor any more. Our NKVD salaries are good!"

Yuri looked at her as if he had never met somebody as stupid and shook his head:

"Silly girl! If we get the State to pay, I can hire a car and we can go out in evenings and have a wild time! What do you think?"

"Hm. It sounds good. Let me think about it."

It didn't take Yulia long to think. Yuri had grown into a tall and well-built officer, though his round face still looked as friendly and childlike to her. She trusted him completely, although she had no romantic notions about their relationship, so she asked her boss for annual leave and, to her surprise, he agreed.

The train journey to the resort of Mamaia took four days, an eternity that they spent playing cards, I

Spy, or avoiding drunks. Snowy stations gradually gave way to windswept ones and then sunny ones.

***

"Oh, it is so beautiful Yuri!" Yulia cried, when she caught her first sight of the sparkling Black Sea. "Thank you! This was such a great idea!"

Yulia bought her first swimming costume and they spent carefree days on the beach. But the normally restless Yuri seemed even more agitated than usual and after only three days, hired a car and told her he wanted to take her on an adventure.

"Alright!" she squealed with delight.

Yuri was able to use his NKVD pass to hire the fastest car in the pool, so they went south, and Yuri drove down the coast to Varna as if the Devil were behind them.

"Slow down Yuri!" Yulia screamed above the roar of the wind in the open-top car. "You'll get us both killed!"

"We're young! We'll live forever!"

At Varna, they turned inland and entered into a dreamy landscape of heather covered moors and lakes.

"Are we ever going to stop Yuri? I need to stretch my legs."

"Yes, we should. Let's find somewhere nice to stop. I have a surprise in the boot."

At a town called Pregrada, Yuri turned into a smaller road with a sign-post for Debelets. They crested a hill and Yuri pulled over.

"Wow! Look at that view! Yuri! It's the most beautiful place I've ever seen!"

The other side of the hill dropped down to a wide lake, on the other side of which stood more hills. A tiny group of houses huddled around its southern edge, but

Yuri felt eager to leave the road. He grabbed a wicker basket and blanket from the boot of the car and led Yulia down a track.

"Is that what I think it is?" she asked, nodding at the basket and giggling.

"It might be. Let's find a nice spot. That rock!"

"Do you remember the fields where we used to play?" Yulia said, sitting on the blanket. "Where we saw the rocket?"

"Yes. Those were good days. I loved you then too."

"Oh Yuri. Don't spoil it."

"Alright."

"Anyway, this place is even more beautiful."

From their perch, they could see over the lake to the hazy, undulating horizon, but to Yulia it felt as if they could see forever.

"Not as beautiful as you," Yuri replied.

They spread out the contents of the basket, a delicious picnic for two. It was 1944, so many items on their menu were rare or unobtainable for most people and Yuri had needed to spent most of his remaining money to treat Yulia.

"Fresh eggs! And cream! How did you get these things Yuri?"

"Call it NKVD power! Ha! I will be promoted soon Yulia. My superior says I have done an excellent job and the apparatchiks have approved his plans for me. I will *always* look after you as well."

"Oh Yuri, you're so good to me."

Yuri wanted to say something, but he pursed his lips. After they finished eating they lay back to bask in the early afternoon sun. Yulia cast a hand over her face and moaned with pleasure, but something soft and wet touched her cheek, so she opened one eye.

"Yuri! What are you doing?"

"Did it hurt?"

"No. You often kiss me, but not like that."

"You're so beautiful Yulia that I couldn't resist."

"Oh. Just the once then. Because we're such good friends. But no more talk of this. It makes me uncomfortable."

"Alright," Yuri replied. "No more words."

He slumped down and remained silent until Yulia grew restless and sat up.

"Let's walk to that big rock there!" she suggested, pointing to a column of striated rock with a flat top that looked as if it had been nibbled right around at intervals by giants. "We can leave the basket here."

"Alright. Race you!"

"But I'm full of food!" said Yulia, in protest.

Nevertheless, when Yuri sped through the long grass, she found her legs pumping as hard as they could to beat him, so she arrived at the rock only a few metres ahead.

"Let's climb it!" she gasped, kicking off her shoes.

"Are you crazy? It's too dangerous!"

But Yulia had already found her first foot purchase and levered herself up with her hands. Yuri followed her. Up and up Yulia went, gasping for breath, often finding no obvious foothold, but each time, she would manage to shift her weight and position enough to find a way forward eventually. For Yuri, the sight of her wiggling bottom became almost too much to bear:

"I think we should go down!" he yelled.

But Yulia continued on. When her hands finally reached the lip of the rock's top, she became impatient and lost her footing. She began to slide down the side of the rock and screamed:

"Yuri!"

But one of her feet suddenly hit something solid. That something shook with the effort, but slowly lifted her until she could lunge for safety on top of the rock. Moments later Yuri's grinning face appeared and he slumped beside her.

"I told you it was dangerous!" he gasped.

"Oh Yuri, you saved my life!"

He put his hand on her shoulder and kissed her again, this time more forcefully. She tried to tell him, "No Yuri!" but his lips suffocated the sound and his weight pressed her against the hard rock.

Yuri began unfastening his trousers. There could be no more doubt in Yulia's mind what was going to happen, but she felt a confused mixture of emotions. She had been raped once before, but because Yuri had been so good to her, she wondered if either she, or perhaps he, deserved, what was coming. She didn't feel so sure about resisting him then. When he released her lips from his own and ripped her tunic buttons off, she gasped for air, but said nothing. When he forced her trousers from her hips and tried to widen the gap between her legs, she even spread them apart for him. She felt partly protective over him and partly grateful for all that he had given her. But most of all, if she closed her eyes, she could imagine that there was something elemental about what they were doing. Telling herself she would say to him after, "Just this once Yuri," she let him have his way, holding on until he subsided, but then found those words would not come. She could only voice her sadness:

"Oh Yuri."

"I love you Yulia! I love you more than anything!"

"Oh Yuri."

She kissed the top of his head, and wiped away her tears before he could see them.

"It really wasn't so bad. Perhaps all women feel this sometimes," she told herself, back in the Hotel.

***

The next day Yuri looked very pleased with himself when he returned from a foray into Mamaia.

Yulia felt angry and about to lose her temper when he kissed her and thrust a small, blue, velvet box into her hand.

"What is it?" she asked.

"Open it!"

She opened the box and stared at a gold ring with a white stone on a bed of satin, the prettiest thing she had ever seen.

"For me?"

"For our wedding."

"Wait! Wedding? I have to think about it!"

"Well think then! I don't have all day. We can get married in the church here. I've arranged it."

Yulia's thoughts tumbled over each other, but she forced herself to think coolly and realised a few important things. Firstly, Yuri would be posted away from her if he were promoted, and they worked in departments too far apart for them to cohabit. Secondly, he had been as gentle with her as he could be when he did it and hadn't hit her. Thirdly, marriage in Russia wasn't simply a matter of status. Every woman wanted to be married, because it gave a woman more protection.

"Alright Yuri. If that's what you really want."

He didn't hit her until Christmas of the following year. Only then did she fully realise what a terrible mistake she had made.

Yes, she was ready to leave Yuri now.

***

Edward's work for the delegation took all day and his team still had more to do when he finally left at 7 pm. He was slashing himself to shreds with guilt over Don's death by the time he left for the Midland Hotel, but this began to metamorphose into a gnawing doubt about Yulia's motives. Moreover, he had begun to feel that everyone was watching him. If he had gone straight to his Suite, he would have sunk deeper into his sense of hopelessness and distrust, and might not have wanted to see her. But she had been waiting for him in the dining room. His doubt vanished and he rushed over to her, but pulled up short. Her face had a large shadow on its left side, impossible to cover completely, even with rouge.

"What happened? Who hit you?"

"Not here. Can we talk in your room?"

"Will Bregovsky let you?"

"Just come with me," she hissed, clearly irritated.

Even during the short distance to the stairs, Edward felt his doubt about her returning:

'Did Bregovsky hit her just to arouse my sympathy? Did she *ask* the Russian to hit her?'

"Why my Suite?" he asked, as soon as he had shut his door behind them.

"Mikoyan is in my room with Kirill and one of the guards – Gregori – now. They have a problem, but it could be good for *us*."

"What?"

Yulia thought his response sounded sharp, so sought an explanation in his eyes:

"You don't trust me, do you?"

"I'm having a hard time. Sorry. It's been a very bad day. I'm doubting everything. Tell me?"

"Not if you are going to be rude."

"Alright. I said sorry."

"They don't have enough shavings. Two of them are virtually identical. 'From the same segment of edge,' Mikoyan said. The other does not give them enough information. Here. Drink this!"

"Oh. I see!"

Edward took only one gulp to down a glass of vodka, which stung his throat and made him grimace.

"That's good then! That means we're off the hook."

"No. But they want yours. Where are they? Are they safe?"

"They're safe. Here." Edward patted his jacket breast.

She stared down into her own glass and swilled its contents.

"Damn! But I guess that's why they didn't kill *me.*"

"They said if you don't give them the shavings, they will kill me and tell Rolls Royce that you gave them the other shavings. I am worried they will kill you too. They didn't say it, but you know too much!"

Edward dropped into a chair and murmured:

"I don't think they would, but … who knows!"

"Don't worry. We will think of something. We have time. They are going soon and leaving the room to me. But let's stay in your room. I will feel more relaxed. At least we can be together, all evening. Don't worry about it now."

"Oh that's just great!" Edward said, getting up and beginning to pace. "So I get permission to be with you in return for betraying my country! I'm not that stupid! Or fickle!"

"Don't look at it that way. I thought you wanted to be with me? This might be our last chance."

Edward looked into her brown eyes and saw the hurt there. He remembered her bruised cheek and took her hands in his, whispering:

"Sorry darling. Yes, let's take the time to think of something. There *has* to be a way out of this mess! And I have to redeem myself somehow for what happened to Don. I can never forgive myself otherwise! But I'm forgetting you. Sit down and tell me what happened. All of it!"

Yulia perched on the edge of the neatly made up bed and began:

"I went back upstairs after seeing you last night and found Kirill in a foul mood. 'Why did you take so long?' he demanded. 'You weren't in the toilet, were you?' Of course, I lied and eventually he calmed down. But then the telephone rang and he left ... . I think he went to Mikoyan's Suite. He was away for a long time. I changed for bed and lay awake, waiting for him. I wanted to sleep, but I feared his mood when he returned. I don't like to be taken off-guard. But he is so ... inconsistent. One day he wants me to be with you and then he is suspicious!"

Yulia stopped and stared at the carpet.

"Then what?"

"Well, I am not sure. I *must* have fallen asleep, because the next thing I remember is Kirill shaking me. 'Wake up you stupid bitch!' he shouted. He told me that, because of me, the British agents are starting to follow ours too closely! Then he told me something about the shavings being no good. He was really angry! At first, I didn't understand what he meant, but then it sunk in. Of course, inside I was happy, but I tried to look sad. I really tried! But he is a perceptive son of a bitch and saw something he didn't like in my eyes. He swore and then yelled –the most terrible yell I have heard from him –

and he hit me with the back of his hand. I almost blacked out!"

"Damned animal. One of these days I will kill *him*!" Edward knelt down, lifted Yulia's chin and stared hard into her brown eyes, asking, "He didn't *defile* you, did he?"

"Defile? Oh no. He would never do that! He's my uncle!"

"Your uncle! That can't be! You told me he was your lover!" Edward jumped up, beside himself. "And! And! You said your uncle molested you!"

"Yes, that's true!"

"But how can this *all* be true! Explain yourself!"

"Stop shouting. If you sit still for a moment, I will tell you."

Yulia had begun to shake and felt the first tears roll down her cheek. But in a strange way she felt relieved to tell somebody about her experience.

Edward stood still, a statue with clenched fists.

"Yes, my uncle touched me, my *other* uncle! And I *didn't* tell you Kirill was my lover. I said being a secretary in Russia has a different meaning to England. Yes, I have been defiled – as you would call it – more than once."

"But you said he's inconsistent? Maybe he's possessive? Jealous?"

"Oh no. No, you wouldn't understand. I'm not sure *I* do. Anyway, I haven't been *defiled* by Kirill. He has such secret thoughts about me, perhaps, but he never touches me. That is why I am happy to be his secretary. Didn't you wonder why we don't share the same Suite?"

"Yes, but I thought he just didn't want to acknowledge you."

"Yes, that is probably also true. He is not so different from other high-ranking officials in the secret services. But anyway, then he said he would let Gregori take care of me. He left the room and the other bastard in my life came in! He was the one who caused this. He hit me with his fist!"

"But you said Kirill slapped your face?"

"No. He hit my arm. Look. He is even more angry than Kirill. I think Kirill told Yuri we had sex."

Yulia lifted her sleeve and show him a large, blue bruise on her upper arm.

"But I don't understand! How can this ... Gregori ... hit you as well! And what's it to him if we had sex, or not! And how the hell does your husband know about all this so quickly!"

Edward's voice had become shrill, and rose almost to a scream as he paced the room.

"Ah! You don't know. Gregori *is* Yuri! Sorry, I should have told you. He made them bring him along, in exchange for allowing me to come. To keep an eye on me."

Edward strode to the bedside table and poured himself a glass of water, a pathetic balm against the black scirocco in his head, but he held up the clear liquid and his anger blew away with a long sigh.

A door shut somewhere nearby and men's voices could be heard. They approached and passed Edward's door.

"They are gone," Yulia said. "Are you ready?"

"I'm confused. But yes. Just give me a moment to collect my thoughts."

Edward looked out of the window, toward the valanced roofs of Derby station, and felt himself falling, falling ... .

When he turned again, Yulia stood at the door, waiting. He nodded, so she led him to her Suite. She cast an expert eye around the large reception room and rearranged two cushions on a chair before declaring:

"There. All ready. No sign of them!" She spread her arms wide and let herself fall onto the chair.

"Let me get you a drink!" Edward declared. "I presume you have vodka?"

Yulia nodded. "I ordered another bottle."

"I need one too. How about food?"

"Yes, I haven't eaten since yesterday. You order. I am exhausted. Do you like chicken?"

"Yes. Let's see if they have it."

***

Edward felt slightly less ill at ease in Yulia's suite, now that he knew Kirill and Gregori's true relationship to her, but he perched on a chair, as if it were a box of dynamite, while he called reception.

"May I order a meal for two in Suite 36? Great. Roast chicken? Alright. Then, may I have that for two with... let's see ... trifle? Yes, coffee, cheese and biscuits. And a bottle of champagne. Thank you."

"When?" Yulia asked.

"Half an hour to forty minutes."

"Well it's only 8 pm; we have plenty of time."

"Yes, but I'm hungry."

"Come and kiss me then."

"Oh wait. We forgot your cheek."

"Yes, but not much we can do about it. I tried to cover it."

"Wait!" Edward called reception again. "This is Suite 36. I just ordered chicken. I know it's unusual, but please can you add a fresh onion, uncut. Thanks."

"Why an onion?" Yulia asked.

"You'll see. Listen, there's something I have to tell *you*."

"What's that?"

"My wife. I think Viktoria suspects. She says she's coming down, tonight or tomorrow. Probably tomorrow, or else she would have been here by now."

"Oh no! Tonight will definitely be our last together then."

"Yes."

Yulia came to a decision and put her hand on Edward's chest:

"Actually, I think I want to tell you something, something else I never told anyone. But it's something you must *never* tell anyone, not even your wife. I will *kill* you if you do!"

Edward's eyes opened wide with shock.

"I don't mean it," she continued, "but please understand, it is not something that is easy to talk about."

"Alright." He placed his hand over hers and felt her raise her fingers, one by one, as she spoke, as if to count off the details.

"It was my uncle. He made a deal with my father. I don't know what, but when he came to visit us – just after I saw the rocket – he tried to touch me. I was milking the goat. And then he … came back later … ." Yulia buried her face in Edward's side. He heard her sob. "He undressed me … by force and … ."

"Alright. It's alright darling. You don't need to tell me. I can guess."

"I can't talk anymore about it anyway." She lifted her face and Edward, watching closely, knew her sobs were real. Her chest heaved, as they only do for somebody out of breath, while tears flooded from her brown eyes. She knew then that she needed Edward, needed him more than anything.

Edward kissed her without holding back and felt all his doubts about her fall away.

"I need you Edward."

"I know. We need each other."

"No, you don't understand. Beneath this skin is a vulnerable girl. Can you understand that? Believe that? I really need you!"

"I think I *do!*"

While they waited for room service, Edward sat on a chair and Yulia sat on the floor, between his legs. He teased her long hair gently with his hands and kissed the top of her head every few minutes, so that she began to feel sleepy.

"Tell me about holidays with Brigitte," she murmured.

"Summer holidays were the best times. But Dorking could be boring during those long weeks. I had friends, but I didn't mix well, so I was closer to Sam and Suzy. Holidays were the best of all. Seems so far away, lost in the past, a bygone age. We always went to Sidmouth until I was about eleven. That's when my mother became ill. I didn't know what was wrong with her, but my father always went away for long periods. The drinks business wasn't so good, so during the previous winter, my father went to America; the company wanted him to establish some clients there. But it didn't go well. He was away a long time and that's when mum got ill. Maybe it had something to do with it ... . But anyway, the following summer my father said we were going somewhere new.

"He had the gift of the gab – that means he was good at talking – and always landed on his feet. Somehow, he had met a rich man who let us stay in his Bailiff's lodge on his estate in the summer. It was free, in exchange for watching the main house when he was on holiday. No doubt there was some dodgy deal behind all this, but that's what father told us!"

"What is a bailiff's lodge?"

"Ah! Well a bailiff takes care of an estate and the lodge is his house. It's small."

"Oh. Carry on."

"It was the place where I climbed the tree. Anyway, the best thing was the swimming pool, but the huge grounds – that's the garden – seemed like a whole kingdom for us.

"Hm. There were three fishing rods and reels in a store room of this lodge. Sammy and I had been begging father to let us use them. We didn't know he could fish. One morning he came out with his pipe in his mouth, wearing a deerstalker hat. He said, 'Come on boys! Who wants to learn to fish?'

"From the first moment, I was hooked! Ha! I didn't mean that pun. It was a hot day on the river, the river where I crossed between the trees. Dragon flies skidded around our heads and swirls of midges followed us until we found a spot with the sun directly ahead. "Never sit with you back to the sun," father told us. "The fish will see you." Fishing is the only genuine thing he taught me. He showed us how to dig up worms, put them on the hook and cast to the runs between green patches of weed. My float bobbed downstream almost faster than I could follow with my eyes. The water swirled and eddied … . You could tell it was a powerful river, but it made no sound. It was hypnotic. Fishing is hunting with the gossamer delicacy of a spider's web. Have you ever fished?"

"Well, Yuri and I used to try and catch little fish with our hands in the river. One day my father made us a net from my mum's old, silk stockings. She was very angry! Ha! We never caught a fish."

"Well *we did*! I caught two trout and Sammy caught something smaller; a gudgeon, I think. 'Blimey!' my ol' man said, when I caught the first trout. 'First time too!' I was so proud. Even Suzy and Brigitte, who brought us sandwiches and pop, thought it was jolly good fun! I went fishing every day until we went home. Ah, that was the best holiday ever! A wheeze!"

"Ha! You sound like a little boy! But is that it? Is there nothing more about Brigitte, kissing or … *love*?"

"Nope. None of that. Not really."

"Not really?"

"Well there was one incident … . Hm. You know what? I have often recalled this incident, but I could never remember how it started! I think I suddenly remembered! Brigitte had taken us on a picnic, the day after another conversation about politics. But now I had got used to those conversations and even enjoyed them, and Sammy and Suzy joined in. 'Sammy, you be a Bolshie and I will be Bour-*geois*,' Suzy declared, as we set up a small table under some trees and laid out cups of tea and saucers of cake.

"Somehow – I don't know – I remember it being a tunnel under the trees; I felt a kind of power in me since bridging the river and I seemed to have tunnel vision. I remember Brigitte looked pretty that day and I only had eyes for her."

"So what did she look like? Was she *very* pretty?"

"Yes … . But not in *that* way, not at first anyway. Wavy, red hair – slightly curly – blue eyes, freckles, slim. I guess she was buxom. And this day she wore a summer dress with ruffed sleeves, but the ruffs were lacy and I could see her arms through the lace. She never showed her upper arms before, so I think she was quite conservative. Maybe she was shy. She had a lovely smile, but frowned most of the time. Anyway, the dress was white, or it may have had a blue, floral pattern – I can't remember. 'You be conservative Bridge!' I declared. But Brigitte teased me and said I should be a socialist. 'Not a national socialist then?' I countered. 'Or a Liberal,' she added, making a rare smile in my direction.

"'Of course, I'll be a Whig!' I replied, showing off the knowledge that I had gleaned from Brigitte. 'Oh such a lov-erly, sweet day,' Suzy said in her most clipped English, holding a cup of freshly poured tea with her little finger raised. I glared at Sammy, who replied gruffly, 'What's sweet about it. Workers died to bring you that tea. I only want water.' I can't remember much of the rest, until Bridge asked me, 'So Sir Archibald Sinclair, I hear you just returned from Berlin. What did you think of it?' I replied, 'Oh, I loved the Brandenburg Gate; a great piece of neo-classical architecture!' in my most pompous voice, forgetting completely my character. 'And how did you vote in last year's Election?' Brigitte asked. 'Why, for stable prices in fishing and farming, and an increase in the number of teachers,' I declared. 'And you?'

"Sammy and Suzy must have been lost, for they just gawped.

"'Foreign policy must not be left in unreliable hands!' Brigitte replied. She did her best to ape – I mean mimic – Winston Churchill's mealy-mouthed delivery, but, with a German accent, it was incredibly funny and had us in stitches! She continued in the same voice, after peering slyly at me, 'So Sinclair, you believe good teaching is essential?' I replied something like 'Yes.' Sammy and Suzy were falling off their chairs laughing, but I could feel the debate had taken a serious turn.

"'I have a teaching degree, but when I go back to Germany, I will not be able to teach,' Brigitte said in her own voice. 'Because you are a woman?' I suggested. My father always railed about female teachers. 'No, because the National Socialist government sacked all Jewish teachers two years ago, and now no Jew can teach.' Sammy and Suzy stopped laughing. We knew what a Jew was. I had expected Brigitte to *challenge* me, but this was different.

"'I'm sorry,' I offered. 'But what are you going to do about it Mister Torrens?' she asked me. 'I will find a way,' I replied. I leaned forward and took her hand in my own. I shouldn't have. My touch elicited a single tear from her blue eyes. The tear rolled down her cheek. 'I will build the fastest aeroplane and take you to Palestine,' I blurted. She squeezed her eyes shut, and another tear followed the first.

"In that moment, I wanted to kiss her red lips more than anything in the world, but I knew somehow that I had been offered, and lost, the chance. I wanted it back so much that I sprang up and ran to the Climbing Tree."

Edward paused, but Yulia had become intoxicated. As she listened to Edward's soothing voice she felt herself fall, almost to sleep. And yet an edge in the otherwise perfect elixir, like a fruit rind, captivated her most.

"Sam and I had flattened the stinging nettles around the base of this climbing tree two days before. It was an ancient elm, which divided into two, a few feet up, to form a natural bowl, and old vines wrapped around its green trunks. It was the easiest tree! So, I rapidly scaled it. I don't know what I was thinking. Sam followed me, shouting, 'I'm going up too Eddie!' and Suzy tried, but she was too young. She suddenly cried out, fell and landed on her back among the stinging nettles. Of course, she tried to get up, and stung her neck and the whole length of her arms and legs. She cried.

"Brigitte didn't know what to do, but *I* did. I jumped out of the tree, over Sam and Suzy's head, and ran to a patch of dock leaves nearby. I gathered up an armful, ran back and rubbed them as hard as I could over Suzy's neck, legs and arms. She looked funny! She was as green as a frog, but the pain quickly subsided and she grinned like a fool.

"That's when Brigitte talked about stinging nettles and I held her waist. Remember?"

"Yes. I was drifting off."

At 8.47 pm, Edward and Yulia heard a knock on the door and he answered, taking the huge tray carefully from the waiter.

Edward lifted the lids on the two plates of food and nosed the roasted chicken bouquet.

"Mm. Smells wonderful!"

"What about the champagne? After?"

"I don't *know* if it goes with chicken, but I don't care!"

The champagne cork came out with a satisfying bang, but Edward didn't manage to stop the fizzing liquid run across his wrist. He licked it off his salty skin greedily.

"Here you go Princess!"

"Thank you sir! Mm. That's nice." She savoured the feeling as the drink slowly trickled down her throat and warmed her belly.

Throughout the meal, Yulia kept glancing at the unpeeled union, lying on a plate. They were in no hurry to eat, and toward the end of the meal, the setting sun cast a rosy light on the wall behind Yulia, adding an air of warmth to their feast.

***

When Yulia and Edward had finished the coffee and round of cheese and biscuits, Yulia slumped back on her chair:

"I am *full up!*"

"That was delicious!" Edward added.

"Are you going to explain the onion?"

"Yes. Go into the bathroom and wash off all your makeup."

"Yes sir!"

When she had gone, Edward sat on the bed, took out his penknife and sliced the onion down its middle.

The bathroom was ensuite, so Edward could watch Yulia while he waited, holding half of the green onion by its crackly, brown skin.

"Do you normally watch women in the bathroom?" Yulia asked his reflection in the mirror.

"I used to watch my mum."

Yulia giggled. She wiped her face dry and presented it to him for inspection.

"Good. Now sit on the bed. Tch! That bruise is nasty. Stay still!" he placed the flat side of the onion's hemisphere against her cheek and began to rub with circular movements.

"Are you polishing me?"

"You don't need any."

"Ha! How did you learn this?"

"It was a home remedy that my mum used."

"On herself?"

"Sometimes."

Yulia let the rare intimacy hang in the air. It floated away on the evening's love.

"How did you get this?" Edward said, touching a small scar on the inside of her arm.

"I fell out of a tree!" she replied, giggling. "My eyes are watering! Can I wash it off?"

"I'll stop now. Leave it for five minutes."

"Alright. "Edward?"

"Yes?"

"I have a birthmark too. It's very large. Like a frog, on my back."

"Oh. I'm sure it's pretty."

"Nobody ever saw it before, not since I was very little. It's grown."

"Let me see."

Yulia pulled her blouse out of her skirt at the back and lifted it, until Edward could see the brown mark. He caressed it with his fingers so gently that Yulia knew he didn't mind it. She almost wept.

"It's good to know you're not completely perfect!" Edward joked. "I was beginning to feel intimidated!"

"You don't mind it?"

"No. And it doesn't look like a frog. It reminds me of Africa."

"Oh!" Yulia giggled. "You said 'used.' Is your mother still alive?"

"No. She died. She died shortly after that last summer at the big house. You know what? I just remembered its name; Silvertops. We went there one last time, at Christmas. I don't remember his name or face, but the owner invited us. It's been just a blank until now, because my mum died a few weeks after. Now, all I can remember is a huge Christmas tree in the centre of a large room and everything, including the door and windows, covered in silver tinsel, making the room look like a frosted paradise. The tree was completely silver, heavy with balls of every shape and colour, purple teardrop, round red, cutaway silver, and topped with a golden-haired Angel."

Yulia stared at the bed before sighing and asking:

"What happened to Brigitte?"

"Didn't I tell you? She married Sam!"

"*No!* Really?"

"Yes. She and her sister were sent out of Germany in 1938 by her parents to stay with a distant relative in London. The parents planned to come, but they left it too late. We never heard from them again. In 1939 Brigitte and her sister were interned, but released about six months later. Two years later she sought out my father, who still lived in the old house at Dorking. She wanted work as a cleaner and he took her in. By this time, Sam was studying engineering too, in London, but he visited often and they struck up a close friendship. Just last year they decided to get married!"

"Wow! That's wonderful!"

"Ha! Yes. He is hopeless with most things, but a regular Rudolph Valentino with women!"

"Do they have children?"

"Not yet."

"And you?"

"None."

"Oh. But you love Viktoria?"

"Yes, but not in the way I did when we met. She had an affair. She gets bored easily, is always looking for more excitement – more everything! She thinks I should be more ambitious."

Edward fetched a wet flannel from the bathroom and wiped the onion juice from Yulia's cheek. The light had almost completely gone from the window, so he peered at Yulia's cheek from very close. She could feel his breath on her neck.

"I can't see if it's working. Should I rub some more? How does it feel?"

"Your touch is very gentle. You are like a doctor."

"Ha!" He let go the onion and it fell to the carpet before the skin came loose and the white hemisphere rolled away.

"Don't laugh at me."

She peered up at him, so that he could see the great sadness in her, just like a child who has been beaten. He couldn't stop himself. Her lips yielded like rose petals, red, moist and innocent. From a great gloom came a greater desire, and from a forgotten heaven came a remembered remedy. He knew there could be only one way to save her now.

"Yulia, *I* love you. *I* need you."

He reached behind her and unfastened the top button of her dress. The moment felt uncannily heavy to Edward, as if his spirit and actions had been weighed, but the verdict not given. He hesitated, expecting chastisement, and sucked in a lungful of air, knowing it might be his last, but Yulia reached up and tugged at the shoulders of her blouse until he could pull it over her head. She released the top button on the rear of her skirt but gave up at the second.

Edward released the obstinate button, and the third. At each stage Yulia tugged more insistently on her skirt, until at last, it slipped from her hips. She stood, shimmied out of the second stage of her chrysalis and stepped free. Edward unclipped her bra and kissed the delicate wings of her shoulders. She seemed to shrink to his eyes, not in fear, but into a little girl, but when he gently turned her she flung her arms around his shoulders, she kissed him hungrily.

"Oh, yes." she murmured.

Her lonely nudity bothered him, so he pulled apart his tie-knot, unfastened the top two buttons of his white shirt and hauled it over his head, not needing, for once, to explain his boyish shortcut.

Nature has no greater mystery than love. Perhaps they didn't undress at all, but were magically transported to the bed, fully fledged lovers from some dream's egg. Yulia found herself riding that old bicycle again, watching that rocket's arc, filled by its fiery power. All these images and more lay themselves upon her sight, until she found herself staring down into the blue spheres of Heaven, and crying out the name of the sky, earth and her destiny:

"Edward!"

Their bodies moved like supple animals, writhing through the mists of time. He barely knew what he did as he sought to lick and kiss every inch of her body, her magnificent breasts, her hips, the curve of her thigh and her ruby red lips.

When he entered her, she moaned, "Yes," but arched her back as if suffering some rictus of agonising ecstasy that she could not endure and he could not share. He almost stopped, but she moaned like a child, a child wanting more, wanting to be rocked to sleep. Edward surged on until he was spent on the crest of a giant wave that took them into the shore and a safe harbour.

He had seen the tears that had fallen from her melted chocolate eyes and each tear had burned him, but it was he who finally realised they had arrived, when his spirit folded its wings and shrunk back into the silken husk of his body.

"Baby! Are you alright?"

Yulia slumped over him, sweating, heaving, wanting no more.

He listened to her pant until her breathing became steady and deep. She had fallen asleep.

***

Edward lay with Yulia upon him until Derby's slim nightlife had died. A cool breeze touched her skin, waking her.

"How long have I been asleep?"

"An hour."

"What time is it?"

Edward looked at his watch.

"Nearly ten."

"Are you hungry?"

"No."

"Tired?"

"No."

"Put the light on."

Edward waited for her to move away and levered himself off the bed. He turned on the light and watched Yulia pad into the bathroom. She took a quick bath and returned, still completely naked.

"You look unbelievable," he told her.

"Like a witch?"

"Like a goddess."

She smiled and again her smile reminded him of something.

'Perhaps Sam,' he thought. The thought endeared her to him even more as he watched her lay on the bed. The thought of divorce, so fleet, had vanished into the mist of guilt when Viktoria had called, but it had left a mark, which he saw as clearly now as a footprint in snow.

"What if I wasn't married in ten years' time?" he said.

"But there is Yuri. I can't."

"Oh."

Yulia sat up, laced his fingers with her own and whispered:

"I would if I could. Maybe. Ten years is a long time. I will think about it. Alright?"

"And you have no children?"

"No."

"I just wanted to know. Come and lay here darling. We have some time. And we have to solve that problem, eventually!"

Edward cast himself upon the bed, so she rolled onto her back. He kissed her and tried to tickle her, making her wriggle enthusiastically before reaching up to kiss him.

"Tell me more about what happened?" he asked.

"When?"

"I assume your uncle did *assault* you, and not just touch you. I ... wouldn't normally ask, but we might not get so much time together again. Please ... I need to know. I care for you too much, *not to* know."

"Oh. Well there is not much to say. I never liked him, but he was richer than my father. I bought that football from him to get the village boys to like me. Shortly after that, and the rocket, he came and promised my parents something – money or a goat, I am not sure. Then he gave me a red ribbon. In my bedroom. I told him it wasn't my colour, but I didn't want to be rude. I hoped one day to live with him in Tosno and move up in the world. Anyway he grabbed me and ... well ... . I don't want to think about the rest."

"Alright." Edward leaned over and kissed her softly on her lips.

"You are not angry with me?"

"Angry? Why would I be?"

"I don't know. I blame myself. It's a guilt many women experience. I think even the many thousands in Berlin will keep silent about it."

"Really? You mean from the end of the War?"

"Yes. We did it. They deserved it for the way they treated us during their advance. But I am not proud of the Russian women who conspired with the soldiers."

"Which Russian women? Soldiers? I've *heard* of them ... ."

"Not just soldiers. Didn't you know that two Russian women achieved the rank of General? In fact, *I* worked on rockets too, in a way. I worked on the production line for katyusha rockets that helped Russia beat Adolf Hitler."

"You mean; helped the allies – America and the British – beat Hitler."

"No. It was Russia that beat him in the Battle for Berlin. The Americans and English were too scared to fight there, street to street."

"I don't know about *scared*!"

"And Russian girls fought there too! Another one of them will be a General soon!"

"Well I ... I ... . I don' know what to say! I've never fought in a war. I never had to serve!"

"Well don't criticize what you don't know. Even our women are braver than your men!"

"Hey! That's going too far! I heard that the American and Brits did a deal with Uncle Joe. That's why we didn't fight there! He *wanted* Berlin!"

"Well, maybe! But don't tell a Russian woman she doesn't know anything about fighting. Some of my friends fought in Berlin and I would have too if I had not been told to work in factories!"

"Oh."

"Don't worry. I am sure you would not have been a coward. But it seems your country doesn't care about women as much as I thought! There is no freedom for women here if they cannot even study engineering! How will there be Russian kosmonavt?"

"Kosmonavt?"

"In space!"

"Oh astronauts."

"Whatever you call them. And how many front-line women pilots do you have?"

"Oh. None, actually."

Edward felt humbled and slightly humiliated by a woman who knew more about War than he did.

"Sorry," she said. "I was carried away. But I tell you one thing. I probably wouldn't be happy in England. We might have terrible things for women in Russia, but at least we can become rocket engineers. Women here seem to be no more than housewives!"

Yulia swung to sit on the edge of the bed. Her jaw jutted like one of those Russian State statues. This was an alien world to Edward and now he began to see another side to Yulia, a side that made him feel inadequate, so he tried to bring her back to their present predicament:

"What are we going to do about the ... you know."

"In a moment. I haven't finished. I was going to say that your Government must like the way our Russian society works, or else they wouldn't be giving us these engines. Maybe they even admire us?"

"Oh! Yes, I suppose so."

Now Edward felt completely out of his depth. He looked at the floor disconsolately until Yulia cut in:

"I suppose we *should* think about what to do now!"

She didn't seem as concerned as he would have liked and the thought lurked in his mind that she might be prepared to leave him and go back to Russia.

They both tossed ideas around. Edward preferred to pace, but the thought of her leaving him so easily niggled.

"You don't seem to be trying so hard!" he declared.

"I am! I just can't think of anything!"

Edward continued to pace, but he became increasingly angry. His frustration at not having an answer, combined with his feelings of inadequacy, stoked his anger to white heat. He noticed the ring on her finger again and lost control of his emotions:

"And what about Yuri? Maybe I'm a fool. Maybe he knows exactly what's going on and you're deceiving me!"

"What do you mean?"

"Do you love him?"

"I told you! No!"

"Then why don't ... *won't* you leave him!"

Yulia stood and paced the room furiously:

"That is all you want, isn't it! Just for me to lose everything to satisfy your ego! I am already risking my life! This ring means nothing to me anymore. I don't even know why I continue to wear it! It's fake anyway!" She pulled it off and threw it at him. "There you are!"

Edward felt shocked at his own loss of temper, because it rarely happened. With a gasp, he wiped his brow and picked the ring up:

"I'm sorry! I'm just frustrated. Hm. It's a very good fake. Looks like a real diamond to me!"

A light flicked on in Edward's mind. He recalled thinking the shavings were as precious as diamonds and realised he might have a solution.

"Wait a minute!" he said. "I think I have it! Yes, it's so obvious!"

"What? We better get dressed. And I am going. Kirill will return soon and I don't know what will happen if Yuri finds us like this!"

Yulia's rage showed on her face, so Edward dare not stop her as she dressed to leave.

"Put your clothes on!" she told him.

"I'm sorry Yulia. I don't know what came over me!" He began to put his clothes on and had just fastened his trousers when the Suite door burst open.

"Yuri!" Yulia screamed. "No!"

The Russian stormed into the bedroom and grabbed her wrist:

"You bitch! You whore! You and Kirill promised me! You *promised*!"

Edward tried to stand up and defend Yulia, but the Russian slammed him back onto the bed again, yelling:

"If you've touched her – and I'll know – if you've fucked her, I'll kill you both! Come on!"

Yuri dragged Yulia, sobbing, from the Suite.

***

Artyom Mikoyan gripped his mug of black coffee and scowled through its steam at the frosted glass of the control tower. He grunted once as Vladimir Klimov brushed his hair back and sat down, throwing his fur hat on the table.

"Are we ready Vladimir?"

"Yes. All's ready. In five minutes, comrade Yuganov will begin the take-off run."

Klimov's breath came out in white clouds. It was 31 December, 1947.

"You're sure, even in these cold temperatures, that the bearings will be adequate for the bigger rotor?"

"The air is denser, that's true. But I don't anticipate vibration, or greater load in *any way*. I'm sure it will work fine. Stop worrying Artyom. Haven't I always been right?"

"Not always, but enough, enough."

"There he is!" Klimov rasped, pointing.

"We must go outside. I want to see everything."

"Alright Art. I forgot my gloves."

"Stick your dainty fingers in your pockets then. If this works, I'll buy you a bottle of the very best vodka today!"

"You're too generous my friend. Let's go."

They both tracked the red and green, blinking blurs from the aircraft's navigation lights, through the frosted window, as the prototype of their new swept wing jet fighter crawled onto the main runway in the heavy fog.

In America, or anywhere else in the world, no prototype would be flown in such weather, but in the Soviet Union, all military equipment had to work in all weathers and temperatures.

When he felt satisfied that everything worked properly and that no sudden gusts of wind were likely, pilot Viktor Nikolayevich Yuganov spoke into his radio microphone:

"I'm ready for the take-off of S-01."

"You are clear for take-off Test Flight S-01. Good luck."

Yuganov settled into his seat, tested his seat straps one last time and pushed the throttle all the way forward. Inside the jet's stubby fuselage, the modified Nene engine spun up to its maximum of 12,300 rpm with a screaming roar.

Yuganov held his foot on the brakes. He could feel the little fighter strain forward, bucking on its rubber tyres. When he felt that he had held it back long enough, he took his foot off the ground brakes and let the fighter roll forward. Faster and faster, through slush, fog and heavy flakes of snow, it hurtled toward the end of the giant runway, and when Yuganov applied the gentlest backward pressure on the stick, floated into the air. He laughed at the aircraft's easy nature, comparing it in his mind to the best girl he had slept with. He banked the aircraft into a wide, climbing turn and vanished from the eyes of those watching. "It worked Vladimir!" Artyom yelled, throwing up his arms and embracing his friend. "It was beautiful. I might even throw in a cigar!"

"Thank you Artyom," Klimov replied, sniffing and allowing himself a thin smile. "But we don't know about the performance yet. Will the new engine work as we hope?"

Chapter Five

E dward changed into his last clean shirt and trousers in his Suite and took breakfast in the dining room. He hoped that by spending time in the crowd he would begin to distance himself from Yulia in the eyes of those who were watching. Two men, alone at their tables, seemed to eye Edward furtively. He resisted the urge to smile at them, instead spending his breakfast planning what he had to do.

A waiter came up to him and leaned close to his ear, whispering:

"There were several calls for you last night from somebody called Sam Torrens. He left a number."

Edward took the slip of paper from the small silver platter and pocketed it, thinking:

'Sam too? I guess dad gave him my number. Wonder what he wants!'

On the way to the Rolls Royce factory, he went over his plan one last time after pressing his breast pocket to make sure that the handkerchief containing the shavings still rested there.

Stepping out of the limousine, he started the short distance to the main entrance, but a man in a suit fell in closer beside him than felt comfortable.

"Mister Torrens."

"Oh, it's you!"

"Keep walking and don't look at me. One of the Russian agents is not far behind. You must *not* see Yulia Panedolia again Edward. You are too close. We think you have something from her, maybe money? I would search you now Edward, but that's not possible." The Vapour moved away to a more comfortable distance.

"Mister Torrens to you."

Edward kept walking.

"I am forbidding you, with direct orders from His Majesty's Government, not to speak with her."

"Oh really? Your lot have made a fine mess of things so far. And you haven't helped me one bit!" Edward had already decided that he had been far too trusting in his dealings with M.I.6 and that if he saw The Vapour again, he would go on the attack. "As a matter of fact, I do have something from her. The Russians stole some metal shavings from the factory." Edward took out his handkerchief, realising this could be the perfect opportunity to get rid of the precious shavings.

"No! Not here. Wait. In a moment, I will ask you for a light and turn to face you. Stand still, so I can shield you, and then put the objects in my breast pocket. Are they small enough?"

"Oh yes."

The Vapour stopped and moved to the side of Edward that faced away from their pursuer. Edward pulled out the handkerchief, poured its contents into his palm and dropped them in the man's breast pocket.

"You will find those very interesting," Edward added.

"How did they steal them? Did you help them?"

"No! I have just spent the last week trying to get them back! You idiots! You didn't even see them take the shavings. I *did*! And your men have been tailing the Russians so closely, they almost pulled out, taking the shavings with them! Then we would really have been stuffed!"

"Yes, that's true! We had to back off. Alright. I'm leaving. If you're telling the truth, thank you. Good bye."

The Vapour peeled away and stepped over the approach road to a waiting black Morris.

Edward arrived at his desk and dropped into his chair with a huge sigh.

"Well, that's that! Nice work Edward!" he told himself.

He sat still, thinking, for some time, before he pulled out his wallet. It wouldn't be the best timing, but he had decided to tear up and discard the photograph of Ewa, because he felt he had to prove his feelings to himself in some way. However, when he looked at the photograph, he saw that it had already been torn into four, jagged pieces.

"Yulia!" A surge of anger rose, only to be replaced by a laugh, deeper than Edward had known for years.

Closing the wallet, he changed into a white coat and made sure its large pockets were completely empty. Taking a deep breath, he reached for the door handle and stepped back. Through the door stepped the remainder of the Nene Team.

'Smutty' Smith, whom he had made Don's temporary replacement, walked to Edward's desk and stood there, waiting for something.

"Yes?" Edward asked, getting the horrible sense that he stood in the dock for a crime.

None of the men returned his friendly gaze.

"Reporting for the meeting sir!" Smith growled.

"Meeting?"

"Final meeting. All the crates are ready for loading now sir. What time do the three trucks get here?"

"Oh! I had forgotten. Sorry, it's been a busy week!" Edward looked for a reaction and saw only the thinnest of smiles, perhaps even a sarcastic one, touch the edges of Smith's lips. He could imagine dark words passing among his men about Yulia having something to do with Don's death. Yes, Edward did stand in the dock. He nodded to himself, but he had no time for a defence now. He shuffled his papers for the collection itinerary, found it and read:

"Arrival of three trucks … 11.10 am. Unload and load crates at 2.30 pm. Lock up the trucks at 4pm." He smiled at the mob, adding, "Management efficient as ever. Looks like they sent some stuff from London on the trucks, so we have to unload that too!"

"Us sir? But we're not *navvies*!"

"Yes Smutty, but you know what Sanderson is like. Efficiency is everything." His attempt to win back some allies failed completely.

"Yes sir. Anything else until then?"

"No. I suggest you all take a long tea break at about 10.30."

"Yes sir."

Even this final peace pipe found no takers.

Edward felt only relief as the men trooped out of his office, because the tea break offered the ideal opportunity to pick up the new shavings. Fetching a packet of Plasticine from the stores, he stuck a wad of the clay-like substance on the sole of his shoes and practiced picking up small items like tacks and screws. The method worked.

At 10.35 he left the office and made for the old machine shop. Standard allows were machined there, but the lathes and mills, which had seen better days, now stood silent. Edward had no trouble walking around one of the lathes until he felt his shoes become encrusted with shavings. Feeling as if he were crunching glass, he walked awkwardly back to his office.

Placing three of the shavings in his handkerchief, he wrapped it around his spare spectacles and put it in his case, reminding himself:

"If anybody *did* see them there, they won't know I have removed them!"

Neatly folding a piece of paper to form a tiny envelope and putting it in his pocket, he pressed more Plasticine into the soles of his shoes. Standing up to leave for the new Nimonic 88 alloy lathe, he almost walked into Sanderson, who stood in the doorway.

"Edward! Good to see you. May I come in for a moment?"

"Um. Of course."

Sanderson didn't hesitate to take Edward's only chair. He played with a pencil on the blotter before beginning:

"Stanley Hooker just called me and told me what a great job you've been doing, eh?" Sanderson's blatant wink told the young manager that M.I.6 had already spoken to Hooker about the shavings. Edward wished he had a seat to recline in and gloat but, he could only shift his weight to his other foot and grin.

"I want you personally to supervise the loading today," Sanderson continued. "And guess what? Mikoyan says he likes you and wants you to escort the loads to the Victoria Docks. I don't know how you managed that!"

"Well. I'm flattered!" Edward replied, hiding the feelings of dread that this prospect opened in his heart.

"But there are two other little matters we need to discuss! Firstly, your wife's here! She's at the main gate and won't be turned away. Hooker says the situation is very delicate and I must get you out of here. That leads me to my second point. How would you like a round of golf?"

"But I have too much to do sir!"

"Nonsense. Come with me. You've earned it. Anyway, we need to get you away from that harridan of yours! Later, I have to take her to dinner apparently! Hooker's idea too. You owe me a round for *that*!"

Edward hung behind Sanderson on the way to the car and prayed that the Plasticine wouldn't come off within anyone's sight. He had to lie flat on the seat as Sanderson drove out of the gates at breakneck speed.

***

Yulia sat in one of the open spaces in one of Moscow's many microdistrict housing blocks.

"Don't go too far!" she shouted.

A little boy, sporting a mop of dark hair, wrestled with a tricycle and shrilled:

"I won't mummy."

The spring flowers had already pushed their way out of the thin layer of soil above the permafrost, drawing Yulia down from the sandy building behind her. A gift from the secret services, her flat had a bathroom, toilet, a separate kitchen, lounge and even a Mediterranean arch, which she could touch if she leaned out of the window. She would add it to the letter she was composing in her mind.

The boy sang to himself while he veered haphazardly along the path between the flower beds. Yulia waited for him to circle a big birch tree and come back to her, before shouting:

"Come and have your photograph taken!"

"Oh *no*! Do I have to?"

"Yes. That's why mummy cut your hair!"

Yulia took the cheap camera that she had recently purchased out of her pocket and made sure she had wound the film on. The boy stepped off the tricycle, planted his fists on his hips and pouted.

"That's not very nice!" Yulia told him. "Smile!"

"No!"

"Please. For mummy?"

"Oh alright. Only for a second?"

"Fine. I will get it."

He gave her a broad grin for almost half a minute, after which he attempted a cartwheel and failed.

"Got it!" Yulia shouted.

***

Faced with the challenge of learning golf at the worst possible moment in his life, Edward Torrens applied himself as best he could. Sanderson wasn't amused.

"You play like a nincompoop Torrens!"

"Sorry sir. I really *am* very tired!"

"Well that's no excuse! After all, you *are* an Englishman!"

Not quite sure what that meant, Edward struggled on until they reached the nineteenth hole, a beer in The Masons Arms.

When he had finished the second pint Edward checked his watch again and interrupted Sanderson:

"Sir. It's 2.20 pm. I really have to get back for the loading."

"Yes! Yes! You're right. Let me just finish this and we'll go."

By the time Sanderson had finished his pint and wove the heavy Rover back to the factory, 3pm had passed. This didn't endear Edward any further to Smith and his crew, who were struggling with the crates on the three waiting trucks.

"We've only loaded two sir! Normally Don drives the fork-lift," Smith explained. "Reggie here's not so good. He nearly smashed a crate five minutes ago."

Edward had noticed the day growing particularly hot during the morning and he could see that the men were covered in sweat.

"Alright. Everybody break for tea," Edward yelled. "I'll find a good driver."

He slipped into his office and began hastily putting more Plasticine on his feet, but Mary poked her head around the door.

"What are you doing? Stone in your shoe?"

"What? Oh! Something like that!"

"Hooker's looking for you. Wants to know what's holding up the loading."

"Bloody hell! Thanks. I'd better get onto it."

As soon as her head disappeared, he took off the Plasticine and found a good driver. Working his men as hard as he dared, Edward finished the loading by 5.10 pm, more than one hour later than planned. The truck drivers had already been waiting in their cabs for one hour and grumbled loudly about the heat and delay. Edward's shirt had become soaked with sweat.

"Okay park 'em in Shed 2! Security will lock up," he shouted to the drivers. "That's all boys. See you on Monday! And thanks!"

Edward ran back to his office and slapped his last wad of Plasticine on his shoes again. Security would not only lock up the trucks, but also do a round of the offices at 5.30 pm, and anybody without written permission to be inside then would be thrown out.

His heart pounded like a freight train as he walked to the Nimonic 88 lathe and paced one circuit around it. Feeling that enough shavings had attached to his soles, he crunched his way back to his office and tore off one of the shavings. He had almost run out of time.

Putting it in the matchbox he added two of the standard alloy shavings he had kept earlier, tossed the wad of Plasticine, still holding some Nimonic 88 shavings within it, into the bin with the other shavings and put on his jacket. He checked his watch; 5.35 pm.

The sound of footsteps approached his door. He thought of switching off the light, but it was too late, so he grabbed the telephone and, like a miracle, remembered Sam's unanswered call. He took out the slip of paper and desperately dialled the number. His door opened and a security guard poked his head around it:

"You about to go sir?"

"Wait? I'm just speaking to Cranwell."

"Right. Back in five minutes."

But the man didn't entirely leave. He hung about just outside Edward's door, his footsteps echoing up and down as he waited impatiently.

"Cranwell?" Edward replied.

"Yes. May I help you sir?"

"Yes. Can I speak to Cadet Sam Torrens please? He left me a message to call. It may be urgent."

The guard outside stopped pacing while Edward waited in silence.

"Sam!"

"Eddie! Is that you?"

"Sure is!"

"I tried to get hold of you all yesterday evening. Dad gave me your number and I have Sunday off. How about some fishing, or something on Sunday?"

"Um."

Edward hadn't thought as far ahead as Sunday.

"Since you're so close ... ."

"Yes. Yes, it would be nice. I might need pepping up. I have no gear though. And no car!"

"Don't worry, I have spares. And I'll find a station for you. Why pepping up?"

"A blonde. Explain later. How's Brigitte?"

"Fine! Fine! She wants to see you."

"Oh. I see. Listen, I have to go. I'll call you early tomorrow evening. Um, I miss you Sam. Look after dad."

"Why so dramatic?"

"Have to go. Bye."

Edward slammed down the telephone, checked his jacket pocket for the matchbox and strode to the door. He turned for one last look around the office and decided that everything looked in order, so closed the door and smiled at the guard.

"Finished sir?"

"Yes."

***

"The Devil's in the detail," his dad used to tell Edward, and he knew it now. The limousine had left the Rolls Royce factory at 5 pm, so Edward could either hail a taxi, try and find a bus, or walk to the Midland Hotel. He chose the last option, knowing the others unlikely to succeed, and quickened his pace. He checked his watch again; 5.47. He would make it, just.

While he walked, he went over what he had done. Never before had he betrayed his employers and he knew he wasn't now, but it felt like it. A cold chill inside him turned his plentiful sweat to an ice bath as he walked and presented a vision of the hangman's noose in the air ahead.

Edward hadn't been able to think of anything other than Yulia clearly and almost broken into a run when he reached the Midland at 6.47 pm. As soon as he knocked, she opened her door, wearing a white dress and the red shoes, almost as if taunting him.

"Thank god! I thought you would never come!" she gasped.

"Yes. Why are you wearing those?"

"Kirill insisted."

"Oh."

Despite his fear, Edward found himself laughing and Yulia joined in.

"They are delayed. They won't be here for half an hour. Did you get them?"

"Did Yuri hurt you? I thought he would."

"No. Kirill persuaded him to calm down, but he stripped me and checked my clothes. We were lucky."

"Thank god. I was *so* worried. You know I said I had an idea?"

"Yes."

"I don't have much time, but here it is. I have gone over it three times in my head and I think it works."

"Well?"

"I hand over shavings, but not the *real* shavings! I give Bregovsky shavings that look like the alloy he wants, but actually they'll be just a very standard alloy. I have them here."

"But he might know they are fake."

"No. I thought of that. I'll give him just one shaving of a new alloy; one even more sophisticated than the one he wants. There won't be enough of it for him to reverse engineer it, but it will certainly intrigue him. He might *even* think he's getting a better deal than before. In any case, by the time he's realised it's not enough to help him, he'll be long gone."

"But wait!" Yulia said. "I don't understand. I didn't understand before and I still don't understand; if they have the alloy, why can't they just analyse its constituent parts? Why do they need more than one sample?"

"Well, without giving away too many secrets, it's the *way* the alloy is used that's so secret. It has to be heat-treated and shaped in certain ways. Some alloys can be milled, or cut, on a lathe and some can't. Mikoyan and Klimov might even think that we're using two different alloys in each fan blade. We actually tried it, but it didn't work."

"Oh. I see. You can't blame me for asking. It sounds like you are taking risks with my life."

"Don't worry. They won't have time to know for certain, thank god!"

"Talk about him, do you believe in God?"

"Well, I'm a lapsed Catholic. I waver. And you?"

"I believe in Titanicon!"

"Who's he?"

"My own god. But probably just the same as yours. It's just that now would be a good time to pray."

"Yes. Don't worry. I wouldn't risk your life. Everything will be alright."

"Are the real shavings still safe?"

"They were in my office drawer and somebody went through it. Fortunately, they didn't find them, but I had to transfer them into my jacket. They've been in my jacket since yesterday. We have another problem!"

"Oh no! There *can't* be anything more. I don't think I can take any more!"

Edward took her hands in his:

"My wife's here!"

"Oh no! Where?"

"Don't worry. She's checked in, but Hooker took care of it. He ordered my boss to take her on a guided tour of the factory. She doesn't know it yet, but he'll insist on taking her to dinner after. She won't be back until late, thank god – or Titanicon! After that, you'll have to stay away."

"Okay. I love you very much."

"We will be together. I will wait."

"At least ten years?"

"At least. I don't think it will be that … long."

"Do you want a drink?" Yulia asked.

"I want anything! I haven't eaten or drunk anything, except warm beer, since this morning!"

"Oh! I only have cake and tea! It's our last time together and I thought it would be nice!"

"It will do. What sort of cake?"

Yulia brushed past Edward. He could see the fear in her eyes, so he grabbed her wrist and swung her to kiss him.

"I love you!" he declared again.

"Do you?"

Her eyes questioned him.

"Yes. I do. Very much."

She kissed him back.

"I'm scared Ed … . I nearly called you Eddie."

"You can if you like."

"No. Not yet. I had the Hotel staff make us a cake, as a farewell gift. They seemed only too happy to do it." She pointed to the shelf above the radio, where a large chocolate cake rested on a silver plate.

"Wow! Chocolate! I haven't eaten a chocolate cake since before the War! Well done!"

Yulia lifted down the cake and took a silver knife to it. Edward saw that somebody had piped 'Farewell,' on the top. He also saw a tiny slice, like a door, in the side of the cake.

"Who was *that* for? You're not dieting surely?"

Yulia pointed to the window sill, where a blackbird pecked at some chocolate crumbs. She cut another tiny slice and carried it on her hand to the bird, but before she reached the sill, the blackbird flew into the room and landed on her palm. Edward couldn't resist taking a closer look, but as soon as he stood, the bird flew across the room and into a closed window. It floundered around the room before finding a perch on a shelf.

"Don't move," Yulia said. "You frightened him, but he will find his way out."

Edward tucked into a large slice of the cake while Yulia poured him a hot cup of brown tea.

After Edward had finished his second slice of cake, the blackbird suddenly flew to the sill and cocked its head at Yulia.

"Look at him!" she squealed. "He's still hopeful for more. But I don't want him to get trapped."

They both watched the bird. Its black eye peered at them from every angle, but when they didn't move to offer it more cake, it leaped off the sill and flew across the street.

"He's been coming here for days. Whenever I opened the window he would sit and watch me," Yulia explained.

"You're clever. They won't normally do that!"

"Oh they will if you are patient. Blackbirds are blackbirds, everywhere! Would you be happy living in Russia Edward?"

"No. At least, I don't think so. Why?"

"I just wondered. We could build a life together *there* one day." She smiled the enigmatic smile that so mystified Edward. He wondered if it would be the last time he would see it.

"I thought we would start a family here?" he replied.

"Yes. That would be nice. I imagine us living in that hunting lodge you told me about, where nobody can find us and we can be free."

"You mean Bailiff's lodge! I don't know if it's still there. Or even Silvertops. I meant to go back there so many times, but I never got around to it."

"Yes. And you can teach me croquet and tennis and all the other English sports." She pronounced 'croquet' like 'rocket,' which made Edward smile. "And we can build rockets together! Maybe I can learn to build engines! Yes!" Yulia became very excited and sat up. "Could I work at Rolls Royce? I already learned engineering skills; I can operate a lathe and a mill and use a forge and press!"

"Well I don't know. I went to Imperial College and studied mathematics. I specialised in fluid hydrodynamics, but there were no girls on the course. I don't know why … . It's just not done!"

"But why not? In my country, it is normal!"

"Yes. But not here."

"Well, you have to come and live in Russia then. I couldn't be happy here. It would be a cage. I would be like that trapped bird!"

Edward shook his head slowly.

"You know, if you came to Russia, I could get you work at MiG. Mikoyan would like to have you. Oh but it doesn't matter … ."

"Yes. I am sure he would like me there, but you know I can't come."

"Yes. They will be here soon. I can't believe I am going. I will miss you so much."

"Apparently, I have to come to London with you tomorrow."

"Yes. But we won't be able to talk, just smile and … ."

"Are you crying?"

"A little bit."

"Oh darling."

Edward moved to sit on her chair's armrest and put his arm around her.

"There! There! Don't worry. I'll give you my address, so that you can write to me. We'll be together somehow."

"Are you sure?"

"Yes. Positive." Trying to change the subject, Edward added, "Sam called tod- ... ." but he was interrupted by a soft knock on the door. Yulia jumped up and opened it. A tired looking Mikoyan led Bregovsky and Klimov into the room. All three stared at Edward. Mikoyan slumped in a chair while Klimov sat slowly, but Bregovsky walked straight up to Edward:

"Do you have what we asked for?"

Edward took out the matchbox and handed it to Bregovsky. The stocky Russian slid the compartment open and dropped the shavings into his fleshy palm.

"Like diamonds," Edward said.

"What?"

"As precious as diamonds," Edward corrected. "A man died for them."

Bregovsky's face creased into a crooked smile. He turned and placed the shavings into Klimov's hands, whispering something, after which Klimov stood and left.

"You will be welcome at MiG Mister Torrens," Artyom Mikoyan said.

But the offer sounded empty and automatic, like something rehearsed.

"We will see you tomorrow?" Bregovsky asked.

"Yes. Hooker insists."

"Good. Let's hope the goods are what we require. Say goodbye to the girl, for now."

Edward stooped and kissed Yulia. Bregovsky grinned and gestured to the door. A few moments later, Edward found himself in his own Suite.

***

There seemed little else Edward could do that evening other than hope his plan had succeeded, and deal with his wife. She returned, escorted by Sanderson, at 9.30 pm, her fury almost completely mollified by the lavish dinner she had been given.

"I'm not happy with you Edward, but I've had a fine day. I finally feel like the *wife* of an executive! But you can wipe that smug look off your face! Now I want a bath and then you can treat me to a drink in the bar and an explanation!"

Sanderson raised his eyebrows at Edward and made a diplomatic exit.

Edward needed a bath too. Since he and Viktoria both had separate accommodation, he was able to bathe alone and gather his thoughts, though not without some trepidation on Viktoria's part at leaving him alone a little longer. Putting on a shirt from earlier in the week, Edward went down to the dining room, where he took a table with Viktoria.

"I want to see this Russian witch!" she told Edward.

"Yes dear. Later. I'm starving! I've been working like a dog at the factory. But its nearly all finished. You don't mind if I eat while you drink, do you?"

"Not as long as I can see you!"

Edward ordered the Friday special, fish and chips and washed it down with four glasses of orange juice, but a headache quickly gained its foothold. Just as he finished eating, Edward saw Bregovsky escort Yulia through the lobby. His mouth full, he elbowed Viktoria and pointed with his knife to the lobby.

"What? What?" Viktoria said.

The mouthful of food saved Edward, for otherwise he would have blurted, "Yulia." Instead, he mumbled, "The Russian woman!"

However, by this time the Russians had left and Viktoria only had a vague impression of a slender woman with blonde hair. However, she seemed satisfied by Edward's coolness and settled in her chair like a mother hen on a nest of eggs. By the time they ascended the stairs Edward's head pounded and he told Viktoria he could do no more than lie in bed until merciful sleep took him.

"I'll come to your room and look after you," she said. "I have some aspirin somewhere in my bag."

With little choice but to spend the night with Viktoria, Edward woke briefly to the sound of drums, only to recognise the sound of rain lashing a roof. The sultry weather had finally broken into a thunderstorm, so Edward feebly tried to count the seconds between the flashes and thunder, but he fell asleep again before he finished counting out the first.

Edward could eat little more than two slices of toast at breakfast and quickly left for the factory. Hooker appeared with Sanderson and the Russians in the turning bay, just inside the main gates, and told him:

"You look pale as a sheet man! Have you seen a ghost?"

"No. Just ate something that didn't agree with me."

The three, green trucks were ready and small groups of Rolls staff stood around, awaiting the departure of the delegation.

"Good luck. Here's the fare back." Hooker said, sticking a ten-pound note into Edward's hand, enough for the fare and a good night out in London.

The Russians, not caring about their own comfort, had elected to travel in the truck cabs, to keep a close eye on their merchandise. One of the Russian agents wasn't present, so that meant two passengers for each cab.

"May I go with Yulia?" Edward asked Bregovsky.

"No. You go with Artyom Mikoyan."

Yulia stood so close to Edward that he could smell the minimal perfume she always wore.

"You smell a bit," she whispered. "Make sure you wash your clothes when you get home."

Bregovsky pulled her by the elbow to another truck and Edward followed Mikoyan to the lead truck.

"You first!" the Russian said.

"Can I have the window? I sometimes get car-sick."

"Sorry. Bregovsky's instructions." Mikoyan's smile looked pleasant, but didn't reassure Edward. He climbed to the high cab and tried to keep his right leg away from the gear stick as Mikoyan's bulk pressed against him.

'Why do all Russian men have to be so bulky?' he asked himself.

"Alright Mister Torrens?" the driver said, pulling out his oil-stained itinerary. "Final destination, Royal Victoria Dock, Bay 17. Let me know when you want a break." He turned the ignition key, crunched the big engine into gear and steered the rumbling truck out of the Rolls Royce gates.

Edward wanted to stop at Leicester, but Artyom ordered a stop in a layby further on. The big Russian ran back to the second truck and confirmed with Bregovsky that they should continue. Edward's driver wound down his window, specifically to spit onto the grass verge, just before they pulled away.

"Leave the window down," Edward said. "It's getting hotter."

"Right you are sir! Fresh day though, after the storm."

Edward drank in the scent of cut grass before the diesel engine fumes swamped it.

At Northampton, cramps had set into Edward's legs and brought him to breaking point:

"We *must* stop here!" he demanded.

Mikoyan threw up his arms and said something in Russian before adding, "Alright! We stop!"

The café break proved only long enough to drink a mug of tea, or coffee, and order a sandwich. Edward, who had not eaten much breakfast, took two chicken sandwiches and happily munched them while the trucks rumbled toward London. His headache had almost gone by the time he finished eating, so he felt much better. Folding his arms, he closed his eyes and before long, he had fallen asleep.

The lullaby of the diesel engine's low rumble kept Edward asleep until they pulled up at the dock, whereupon he opened his eyes and beheld the ruins of a bombed-out building. To its right the deformed skeleton of an iron crane stooped in silent supplication. Edward thought it must still be 1940, so he jerked upright in his seat and peered up at the sky in terror.

"We're here!" the driver shouted through his open door. "You slept like a baby! Had a hard night, did we sir?"

Edward ignored the man's sly comment and climbed unsteadily down to the quay.

The Russians all stood in a group, smoking, while a crane began to hoist the crates from the trucks onto a ship. Edward saw a name he could not read on its hull. Somebody had already unloaded the Russian baggage; ten suitcases sat on the cobbles beside them, four blue ones in front of Yulia. He sought out Yulia's face and she smiled back, giving him an instant of sunshine.

Edward suddenly noticed that another agent had arrived and stood deep in conversation with Bregovsky. They both stopped talking and looked at him for a moment. Bregovsky said something brief to the other before they broke apart and Yulia's uncle strode up to Edward:

"We have finished our business Mister Torrens. Thank you very much for your help. You can go home."

Edward felt the rush of relief. He had half expected to be shot, or at least drowned in the murky Thames. After a moment to recover, he suddenly felt like asking many questions, but tried only:

"May I be alone with Yulia for five minutes?"

Bregovsky looked at the ground, sighed and replied:

"As you wish comrade. Five minutes."

Edward assumed the word 'comrade' to be some kind of personal joke, so ignored it.

"Both of you keep your hands behind your backs and stand slightly apart," Bregovsky concluded. Gregori, or Yuri, as Edward knew him to be now, eyed the Englishman when he approached Yulia.

"Hello," she said, as Edward arrived at her side. "Well, this is good bye, for now."

"Yes. I hope, not for long."

"I will always love you Edward. Don't forget it."

"Oh yes, and thank for tearing up that photograph!"

"You are not angry with me?"

"A little."

They both laughed.

"Last crate is loaded!" Bregovksy shouted. "Come on Yulia!"

"Well, I have to go," Yulia said. She stood on tiptoes and kissed Edward.

"Your Kirill will be angry with you. And Yuri even more!"

"Let them be."

"Write to me!" Edward said. "You have my address."

"That will be difficult from Russia." She looked thoughtful for a moment. "Maybe from somewhere else, close by."

A thought came into Edward's head, so he blurted:

"I tried to free you, but all I did was trap myself!"

"Don't worry. Everything will be alright."

Yulia turned and walked back to the group of Russians, wobbling slightly, when the heels of her green shoes dug into the ruts between the cobbles.

Edward smiled and shouted:

"Good bye."

Bregovsky shouted back:

"Have a nice life Mister Torrens."

The Russians turned and walked up the gangway to the ship in single file. Yulia turned once to wave at Edward and was gone.

Edward waited for five minutes, but saw no sign of them. He turned to the trucks and met the eyes of his driver. The man pulled out the itinerary and waved it at Edward.

"Got a pe-..?" Edward asked.

The ship's horn sounded, drowning out the end of his question, so Edward repeated it.

He examined the dirty sheet of paper for any sign of the ship's name or destination. He could find nothing, so scrawled his signature at the bottom and asked:

"Can you give me a lift to a bus stop?"

"I can do better than that sir. We go past an underground station in five minutes. Drop you there."

Edward hadn't felt like taking a good night out in London. He felt like a ghost on the underground and the darkening countryside outside the train window blackened his mood further.

The Midland Hotel had a forbidding feel to it for Edward, but he had one more night booked and had promised to call Sam from there, so he packed and sat on the bed for a moment to think. All his thoughts until now had been focused on keeping Yulia and himself alive. Now the vaporous guilt that had grown inside him over Don's death seemed to expand from him to fill the room. He had to do something for his friend, if only to help Delores.

He wanted to speak to Delores, but he feared her telephone might be bugged. A visit could be even more dangerous. He could arrange to meet her in secret, but that meant writing. The more he considered the problem, the more he realised he had made a mistake.

"I should have asked Mary to type an address on an envelope, so that I could post it from Derby. Now I'll have to do it from Barnoldswick and it might look suspicious! But what am I going to say anyway? I want to give her money. I can give all that I have in my bank account."

Edward spent a long time thinking how he could do this, but each time he came up against the same problem:

"Don and Delores are, were, simple people, but they have their pride. I know Delores won't accept! But I *have* to do this. It's the only thing I *can do* now!"

Not able to come up with a plan, he had a call put through to Sam at 9.59 pm.

"Eddie? It's bloody late chum! Another minute and they wouldn't have allowed it. Have to make this quick. I did a recce and you need to meet me at Radford station on the mainline from Nottingham to Grantham at 7 am. Can you do that?"

"I'll try. Radford at 7 am. Right. See you there."

"Have to go. See you tomorrow Eddie!"

The Hotel rustled up some cold meats for Edward's supper, but he felt too restless to sleep. Instead he decided to avoid any possible encounter with Viktoria and get as far on his journey to Radford as he could that night. He grabbed his suitcase and made for Derby station.

Edward might not have realised it, but his obsession with repaying his debt to Don had more to do with holding down the growing fear he felt for himself and Yulia.

***

Edward's July fishing trip with Sam had not gone so well. Though he had hoped it would take the edge off his fears for Sam, it proved to be the start of his withdrawal from his family, only alleviated by a brief moment, basking in Sam's glory at Cranwell.

"Eddie! Sorry if I'm a bit late! Traffic was awful."

"It's 7.15 you lazy oaf. What sort of discipline do they teach you at that RAF place ... what's it called?"

"Ha! We call it Cramwell or Bramble ... after the jam. Not many pilots crashed recently though, thank god!"

"Anyway, I've only been here half an hour. So, where are we going?"

Although Edward had only just arrived at Radford station, he had in fact spent the night on a Nottingham station platform, sharing a packet of biscuits with three tramps. He felt glad to have arrived.

"River Trent is just a little way down here. Found a great spot. Day tickets. Have you ever caught a big barbel?"

"No. I don't think I have."

"They fight like hell! Beautiful buggers too. Let's see if we can get one. Everything we need is in the back."

Sam led his older brother to his red Austin. Taking a side road, they drove north, until Sam turned left into Stoke Ferry Lane and finally pulled up next to the swirling waters of the Trent.

The sun had risen two hours before, so when they carried their fishing gear along the riverbank, every swim they came to had been occupied by anglers.

"Popular spot then!" Edward observed.

"Doesn't matter. I know the best spot!"

"How's that?"

"Met an old guy when I came here. He told me."

"What are we using?"

"Bread. RAF bread; not the best, but it'll have to do."

They took up position, half a mile further on from the last angler they had seen. A stand of poplars on the far bank waved their topmost boughs in the gentlest of summer breezes, but the blue dome overhead only reminded Edward of Yulia. Even as the golden orb bisected it, he still struggled to recall the magic of fishing as a youth:

"The river looks so calm, and yet so restless Sam."

"Yes. Stop blabbering and set up!"

With the tackle box set between them, they both plugged the split-cane rod ferrules into each other until both extended twelve feet over the brown water. Then Edward took the drum reel and attached the rod's handle to it, pulling the line out through the eyes and along the rod's length. He slid a cork float's eye over the end of the line and tied on a tiny hook, before finishing by weighting the float with four, tiny lead shot.

Instead of a float, Sam attached a heavy lead weight to the line, about twelve inches from the hook. This weight held the bait on the bottom of the river and in one place.

"Where's the bread?" Edward asked.

"In this bag. Let me do it. Needs wetting. Bit stale."

Sam took the half loaf from its paper wrapping and dipped it for a few seconds in the river. He could smell the subtle aroma that always hung around a fishing swim: a mix of worms, bread, old sausage, potato and rotting weed. Somehow it smelled good. He pulled out a wad of bread and rolled it into a ball between his fingers and thumb. Squeezing it tight he tried to insert the hook into it, but the wet lump of bread fell off. He put some more bread in his mouth and chewed it into a tight ball, before squeezing it around the hook. This time it held.

"Casting!" he shouted, before launching the ledger weight into the middle of the wide river and sitting down with satisfaction. Between the reel and the first eyelet, he had slackened the line into a low bow and hooked a cigarette paper over it to indicate when he had a bite.

Time seemed to drift away, like the silently waltzing streamer weed, going south.

"Lunch up!" Sam called, making Edward's face jerk up from its perch on his knees.

"I think I was asleep. What time is it?"

"Twelve thirty. Good job I suggested you should ledger, like me, or else I think you would have fallen over!"

"Sorry. It is just so restful. The heat … ."

"You haven't said a word all day!" Sam said, handing him a cheese sandwich.

"Sorry. I don't know. There just seems nothing to say!"

"That blonde?"

"I guess so."

"Tell me about her. If there's something on your mind ... . I know I'm younger, but does it matter, if you need to get something out in the open? I'm a good listener. I spent all my youth listening to you babbling on!"

"It's nothing really. Another brief romance that didn't go anywhere, due to circumstances."

"And you still look at that photograph of Ewa every day, I suppose?"

"Ha! No. Actually, the blonde tore it up. I threw it away."

"Good. Well that's something anyway. Sounds like the blonde knew a thing or two. Strong willed ... . Yes, I could see her being good for you. May I ask her name?"

"Yulia."

"And the figure?"

"About five feet seven, hair the colour of wheat, brown eyes, figure any woman would kill for. And I admit, I was struck by all that. But that's not all of it. She had, has, more than that. A mind that truly engages me!"

"I bet. Hey, I think you have a bite! Look lively!"

Edward jumped up, put his forefinger on the rim of the reel drum to brake it and whipped the rod tip up in the air from its rest. The line pulled taut and the rod arched.

"You got one!" Sam yelled. "Bring him in slowly."

The line seemed to draw tighter and tighter until both men thought Edward had hooked a giant.

But when Sam scooped up the last bit of line in the landing net, they saw that Edward had only snagged some weed. He knelt down and extracted the line from the slippery green stuff and found a tiny, silver fish on the hook.

"Blimey! A little bleak!" Sam declared. "They don't come much smaller!"

"Well at least I caught something!"

Throughout the afternoon, Edward said nothing. Sam felt that the more he tried to get his brother to talk, the more he would withdraw into himself. Knowing that something had gone seriously wrong, he grew more and more frustrated with his older brother, but nothing he could do or say seemed to draw Edward out. He checked his watch; 6.30. His promise to Brigitte and Susan to get something out of Edward or at least cheer him up looked like failing.

The sun had dipped below the top of the poplar trees, whose wagging branches played tricks with its reddish light. Sam felt about to explode when his rod tip whipped round and twelve feet of split cane almost vanished into the river. He just caught the butt in time and yanked the rod up and back, to drive the hook firmly into the fish's mouth.

"Don't let it go Sam! It's huge!"

Sure enough the fish set off toward the far back like an express train and made the line thrum like guitar string.

"Jesus! This is big. Get the net ready Eddie!"

For half an hour Sam fought the aquatic monster. Both fish and man finally grew tired, but the man prevailed and Sam dragged the death-weary fish over the triangular landing net.

"It won't fit Sam!"

"Just hook the tail in and scoop it out."

But as Edward reached for the bronze fish, luck suddenly came to its aid and the hook pulled loose. Almost too weary to move, the fish slowly flicked its tail once and vanished into the deep.

Both men were too stunned to speak.

"Did you see it?" Sam finally gasped. "Eight pounds if it was an ounce!"

"Ten, I would say. I'm so sorry Sam!"

"Yeah! Well, easy come, easy go. It's the fight that counts anyway. I won't forget that one!"

"I won't forget this day Sam."

"No. Me neither. Well I think we should pack up. I have to get back in time for curfew and I said I'd visit Brigitte first. Until we get married quarters she has to rough it in Sleaford. I'll drop you at Nottingham station."

"Fine."

Sam broke Edward's sullen silence on the way to Nottingham:

"You should visit dad more often Eddie. I know he's an old sod, but he really *is* very lonely. You can't think about yourself *all* the time. Susan and I did our best, but it's you he thinks of most."

"I mean to Sam. It's just that old car probably wouldn't make it ... ."

"*Yeah.* Excuses. Buy a new one like mine. You *have* the money."

"I will do. Anyway, care to tell me how he knew I was in Derby?"

"You know dad. He knows just about everybody."

Sam hoped his brother would bargain, offer him something in exchange for his knowledge about their father, but by the time they reached the station, Edward had still not told him anything more. Sam decided to remain tight-lipped. If he had to go to the grave without telling Edward how hard their father had lobbied Hooker to get his brother the Russian project, so be it.

The first thing Brigitte asked him when he walked in the door was:

"Well? Any luck?"

"No. I caught a *big fish* ... ."

"Oh. Susan will be so disappointed. Do *you* think he has messed up?"

"That's what dad thinks. If he has, he's going to lose his job. And that may not be all!"

"Oh god!"

***

Edward saw the neatly typed white envelope, sliced it open and read the cover letter in the yellow glare of a September dawn:

> You are invited to attend the graduation of Samuel Torrens at RAF College Cranwell.

Also in the envelope, he found the Graduation Ceremony programme, emblazoned with the RAF College, Cranwell coat of arms. At the bottom, he saw the date: 26th September, 1946.

Since the Russians had left in July, Edward had felt a growing sense of foreboding. His fishing trip with Sam had been a gloomy affair, because he had not felt up to talking much about Yulia, but he could think of nothing else himself. The Graduation Ceremony offered a chance to get out and break the monotonous routine of work and also the perfect opportunity to help Don's widow. The only drawback would be the presence of his father.

On the 26th, Edward said an icy goodbye to Viktoria and drove up to RAF Cranwell. He didn't normally use his Austin for long drives for fear of its expiry, but his plan to help Don also required the use of his dilapidated car, so he drove the whole way with his fingers mentally crossed. The moody, overcast sky almost matched the mid-blue of the RAF parade uniforms Edward glimpsed as he made his way across the parade ground to the rows of seats on the grass. Most of the visitors had already sat down, but a few still swirled, trying to find somebody. Edward spotted his father and Susan, talking to a dashing man in the parade uniform, so he ran up and tapped the man on the shoulder.

Sam turned and threw his arms around his brother, exclaiming:

"Eddie!"

"How are you old son? You look dashing!"

"I'm fine."

"Where's Brigitte?"

"She'll be here in a minute. She just wanted to freshen up. Take a seat, I have to go in five minutes. I'm not supposed to be here!"

"I'll stand. It'll be easier for her to find us."

Edward embraced Susan, who had grown into slender woman with finely chiselled cheek bones, and took the waiting hand of his father, Dominic.

"How are you son? You never came to visit and I have been worried about you."

"Fine dad. I can't believe there are so many cars! Who would believe so many new recruits so soon after the end of the war?"

"Life must go on," Dominic replied.

"Are you going to tell us about the Russian goddess you seduced?" Susan cut in.

"Perhaps later. Not now."

"Here she comes," Sam said, indicating his approaching wife with a nod. "I have to go," He pecked Brigitte on the lips and strode toward the imposing college building.

Edward took in the ravishing sight of Brigitte, who wore a simple, white summer dress and matching hat. She shielded her eyes as a sudden beam of golden light struck her face, under the brim of her hat. Her freckled skin seemed translucent in the light and her brown eyes were filled with joy at the sight of Edward. They embraced only briefly, though Edward thought he felt her lips brush the side of his neck.

"You look gorgeous," he said. "This is only the second time I've seen you since we were kids – I mean Sam and I– and you were skinny at the wedding. I prefer you now, with a little more weight on."

"Thank you. That's very courteous of you, under the circumstances," she replied, winking at Susan.

They heard the sound of a distant drum.

"We had better sit down," Susan suggested.

Only ten rows back from the front of about sixty, long rows, nevertheless Edward could only catch glimpses of new officers on the parade ground itself. Instead, the magnificent façade of the College Hall filled his view. Far above the portico, supported by white pillars, soared the white clock tower.

The band struck up a slow time march and somebody murmured, "They're coming!"

The officers, wearing white belts, marched across the parade ground to the drum's beat and marched back in quick time. Suddenly the band stopped. Edward fumbled for his programme, while asking:

"What's happening now?"

"Award Ceremony," his father replied.

"Presented by the King and attended by Air Marshall Sir Arthur Barratt," Brigitte added. "You never were any good at research Edward."

"Ha! And you haven't lost anything of your ability to tease me!"

"Are you better at politics?"

"Sh!" Dominic protested. "I want to hear!"

"Well you must have damned good ears old man!" Edward retorted.

Susan elbowed him in the ribs.

"It's over, I think!" Brigitte announced, five minutes later.

"Grub time now!" Susan added.

They made their way toward the college hall and climbed the portico steps. Brigitte looked around for Sam.

"Sam's flying," Edward reminded her. "He will have gone to prepare."

"Oh. Does it take *that* long?"

"For a display, yes. Everything has to be just right."

"What's he flying?" Dominic asked nobody in particular. Only Edward knew the answer.

"Miles Magister."

"What's that? Fighter?"

"Trainer."

"Oh. Does that mean he's a bad pilot?"

"No."

The large hall filled with hungry guests, who picked their way noisily around silver tureens of soup and cut glass punch bowls. A bustling woman almost knocked Edward's plate of ham and cucumber sandwiches out of his hand.

"Worse than Harrods on the first day of sales!" Edward joked to Brigitte.

"Anywhere they can get a free meal!" Susan interjected.

"Susan is our resident Socialist," Edward added. Susan circulated away, leaving Edward alone with Brigitte. "So what is this big surprise Sam keeps hinting about?"

"Wait and see. It's good to see you Edward. Can't you tell me a little more about the Russian? *Please?* I can even promise not to tell Susan."

"I would rather you *did* tell her. I don't much like talking about it *at all*, so definitely not twice! All I can tell you is that I fell for her and she went back to Russia. Not her choice ... . She had to go. It's just a sad story."

"Oh. Yes, that's sad. You don't seem to have much luck with *women*."

"No. I do with engines though."

"Yes, but you can't marry one."

"Ha! You like marriage then?"

"Why wouldn't I?"

"Sorry."

"No. I'm sorry. I'm still challenging you. I don't know why. What I mean is that Sam's a lovely man. He is kind and enthusiastic. He will make a wonderful ... ."

"Father?"

"Yes. I have no complaints. I only wish he wasn't training to be a pilot. If there is another war ... ."

"Yes. I know what you mean. But I can't see there being one. Nobody has the stomach for it after the last one."

"I hope you're right. Shall we go? I think the display will start in half an hour and we have to find our seats again. I want a piece of that raspberry tart too."

"Yes."

The display started with a fly-by of three, wartime De Havilland Mosquitos. Painted in training yellow, the sleek, piston-engine aircraft elicited a nostalgic sigh from the crowd. Three Miles Magisters followed them, wheeling as they began their display.

"They don't look so good," Dominic said. "Why's Sam in one of *those*?"

"Because they're going to do aerobatics dad. The Mosquito can't do that."

"Oh. Which one is he?"

"The one on the right."

"Is that easier or harder?"

"Harder."

"Oh. At least that's something."

As the 'V' shaped flight of little trainers wheeled around the sky, sometimes in a tight turn, sometimes climbing into a long loop, Edward noticed that Sam held his position more steadily than the other wingman.

"He's jolly good!" he told Brigitte.

"Yes. They say he's one of the best this year."

"Probably *the* best. The only reason he didn't get an award is because of a party he told me about."

"Is that what he told you? No, he overstayed his leave to be with me."

Shortly after the display finished, Sam ran up to them, sporting the clean shape of goggles on his oily face.

"I only just managed to get away!" he told them. "What did you think."

"You were bloody marvellous," Edward told him. "Best pilot today."

"Thanks big brother. I bet you told them something about Yulia? I'll get it out of Brigitte later. Did she tell you the news?"

"No. But I think I might have an *idea*."

Sam nudged Brigitte, but she elbowed him back, so he said:

"Brigitte is pregnant!"

"I thought so. Congratulations to you both. What do you want; boy or girl?"

"Both and either!" Sam replied. Have to go. Catch up with you all later." He turned to Brigitte. "See you on Monday dear. I have a week's leave.

"Have they assigned you a squadron yet?" Edward asked.

"Oh, officers get to choose. I had a choice of three and I chose 616 Squadron, Finningley, Yorkshire. I'll start off on Mosquito night fighters. But the gen is they'll be getting Meteors soon. That's much more my cup of tea! See you!"

"He's just like a little boy!" Brigitte exclaimed, clapping her hands together.

"Little rascal if you ask me!" Susan suggested.

"Always was!" Dominic agreed. "All the same, wish his mum was here to see it."

"How's the drinks business?" Edward asked, as they walked toward Dominic's Rover.

"Ach! It's all dried up. I have only five years to go, but I am practically retired already!"

"Take it easy dad," Edward replied, taking his father's hand again. "I *will* come and visit you soon."

On his fraught drive home from Cranfield in the old Austin, Edward could at least congratulate himself that he had finally managed to post a letter to Delores. The news about Don's accidental death at Rolls Royce had been announced in the Derby Telegraph. He had typed Delores' address on his old office typewriter at Barnoldswick, but posted it from Derby, knowing she would assume it to be from Rolls Royce. The letter explained that he needed to speak to her about Don's death and proposed that he meet her in Letcliffe Park, the following Tuesday, at 7 pm. It concluded by asking her to come alone and bring Don's bank details.

***

Edward arrived early at Letcliffe Park and strolled around its perimeter in his overcoat, trying to look innocent. Rain looked likely and the chill air seemed an early portent of winter. He didn't recognise Delores when a woman in a thick, fur coat and headscarf walked up to him and said:

"Hello Edward. Sorry I'm late. I nearly didn't come."

"Delores. Let's sit on the bench. Sit away from me. I'm sorry about all this, but it's unofficial. Understand?"

"Yes. But why all the cloak and dagger?"

"I'll explain in a moment. How are you?"

"Oh, I am alright I suppose. It's been hard, but you have to carry on, don't you?"

"And Ricky and David?"

"Yes, they're hit worst. I feel so sad for them. Can you tell me what happened? They said it was an accident."

"Yes, I know what they say. I also saw the newspaper report. Listen, Delores, this is really difficult to tell you. First of all, I'm here on behalf of Rolls Royce, but this is very, very unofficial. Do you understand?"

"Oh, I see. I think so. I never was very good at official stuff!"

"Well anything I tell you must be just between us. You must never tell another soul. Unless you understand and agree to this, I can't tell you anything more."

"It wasn't an accident, was it?"

"*Delores*?"

"Yes. Sorry. I agree Edward. I'm good at keeping silent. Go on, I want to know."

"First of all, I have to ask, did Don have life insurance?"

"Yes. He took it out a year ago. The funny thing is that he kept up the payments, even though we were struggling with other things."

"A year ago? I thought it might be more recent. But it's good. I'm sorry I couldn't contact you sooner. I've been very worried about any financial difficulties you might have, but I couldn't contact you sooner. So, you have enough for yourself and the kids?"

"I don't know if it will be enough, but I suppose you know that Rolls has told me I will get Don's full pension. I think that's very generous of them, because it normally ... ."

"Yes! Yes! I know about that. I haven't much time. The company wants you to have another £1000, but it has to be paid discretely into your bank account and not now, but later. Do you have your bank details?"

"No. I don't have those. I want to know *what happened to Don!*"

The pitch of Delores' voice rose, telling Edward how desperately she needed to know the truth. He also felt that she had begun to suspect he knew something and wouldn't tell her, so he turned to face her. He stared into her eyes and saw the grief and pain that flooded out of them. Delores wept, so Edward took a deep breath and told the lie that he had practiced:

"Listen Delores, Don told me about his difficulties with gambling and the mortgage a few days before. I never expected him to do something stupid, but I should have known. I feel responsible."

"It's not your fault. So, that's why he did it? I suspected it. In my heart, I felt it might be that. We got a letter, just before it happened, saying that Don's post was moving to Derby and that Rolls would help us relocate if that was our wish. Of course, with the state of our mortgage, we couldn't sell, so it would have meant the end of Don's job!"

"Yes, I had the same letter, but only saw it when I got home the following Monday. I can't tell you much about it. But I need those bank details. Can you send them to me?"

"But I don't understand why Rolls sent *you*! Why couldn't they just tell me?"

"Because it happened during the visit of some very important guests. Rolls can't afford something like this to get out. That's all I can say! I wish I could say more! Are you going to send me those details?"

"I have them here. I didn't want to tell you until I was sure. Wait."

She took out a scrap of paper and thrust it into Edward's hand.

"I have to go Delores. Don was my friend, perhaps my best friend. I can't tell you how sorry I am."

"I know Edward. Don't worry. We'll be fine."

"The money will go into your account, but it could be any time in the next three years. Now would be too soon. The Government might take a gander."

"Alright. Take care. And don't *you* have an accident!"

Edward felt desperate to tell Delores the truth, but he knew that would put her and the kids in great danger.

"Remember, not a word to anybody!" he replied.

As Edward walked away he whispered:

"Don, please forgive me!"

***

Edward had expected another visit from The Vapour and it came a week after the Cranfield graduation. He had just left the Rolls Royce plant in Derby when he saw a shadow on the pavement in the setting sun. The shadow followed his own very closely for a while, so Edward stopped in a deserted side street and waited.

"Mister Torrens. So good to see you again."

"Really."

"I wondered if you could help us clear up two little mysteries."

Edward sighed before answering:

"What?"

"Well, your little Russian friend left two items behind in her Suite – well, three actually. She left these."

The Vapour held up a photograph of a pair of red shoes. Edward smiled and thought:

'Thank you Yulia!'

"You're smiling. Is it funny?"

"Sorry. Yulia left that to help you. You see, that is how the Russians tried to smuggle out the metal shavings. If you look at the shoes closely, you will see that the soles are very thick, soft rubber. You might even find the impressions of some metal shavings. But the shavings were not enough. I saw her pick them up on her shoes and I kept some that I found in the limousine. They asked for these and we gave them fake ones. They will, no doubt, by now, realise that they've been tricked!"

"I see. You should have contacted me before getting involved."

"I didn't have enough evidence at first, and Sanderson had warned me not to mess up the whole operation. So, I had to investigate myself. Turns out to have been the right decision, because your men nearly let the Russians get away with it!"

"I see. We also found what was left of a large chocolate cake, and underneath it, this." The Vapour held up another photograph, this time of the ring with the white stone. "Can you explain this?"

"Hm. That's personal. It has no meaning other than that she is saying that she is ... will remember me. The ring was a gift from a Russian ... boyfriend. You can keep it."

"It's our property Mister Torrens. How are things otherwise?"

"Fine. If that's all your questions answered, I'm rather hungry, so I want to get home."

"Very well. Thank you for your cooperation, for now ..."

But things weren't very well. Shortly after Edward and Viktoria moved to Derby, she had another affair and both decided to call it a day. They separated and late in 1949, the Decree nisi finally came. Edward felt lonelier than ever.

***

Sam arrived with five other new officers at 616 Squadron in early October, 1946.

His first two years, piloting the twin-engine De Havilland Mosquito, flew by quicker than any other years of his life. The Mosquito was a piston-engine fighter bomber, designed in the early stages of WWII. Known as the 'The Wooden Wonder,' it had been designed to be built almost completely of plywood, making it so light and fast that it needed no protective armament. The Germans had feared its speed and weapon delivery capability, but now it had become outdated. Sam's last flight before converting to the newer, jet fighter, the Gloster Meteor, would be a routine, simulated interception over Cumbria at night.

Sam punched the tyres of his Mosquito absentmindedly, followed on his routine pre-flight check by his navigator, and radar operator, Phil 'Specs' Matthews. The eye-aching white light from a truck spotlight made the aircraft look as if were painted black, whereas, in fact, it had been painted the typical RAF brown and green camouflage above with black underneath. The bulbous nose, which spoiled the aircraft's otherwise smooth lines, housed the latest radar equipment.

"Last Op. in the ol' girl," Specs said. "Don't suppose we will miss the ugly ol' crate."

"Oh, she's not so bad. I like girls with big noses. But I'll be glad to stop flying at night. I want to be up in the wide, blue sky. That's what I joined up for, not stooging around in the dark like a thief."

"Know what you mean. After you."

Sam climbed the short ladder to the nose hatch and slung his parachute onto the pilot seat. Specs followed, and began strapping himself into his own seat.

"Intercept 241 ready for take-off," Sam called into his radio microphone, when he had completed his checks.

"Intercept 241, you are clear for take-off. Runway 2, wind speed across the ground; ten knots. Good luck."

"Thank you Duck Pond Control. Time you were in bed."

"You're the last tonight. Don't come back until 5am, or you won't get in!"

Sam tucked a curl of his brown hair under his helmet, pulled down his goggles and taxied onto Runway 2. He pushed the throttle levers fully forward and the two Merlin engines whisked the light aircraft into the moonless sky.

"Vector 300, 175 knots," Specs said into his microphone. "Flight time approximately thirty-five minutes, allowing for west nor' west headwind of twenty knots at 10,000 feet. Maintain that altitude and we'll be fine. Time now 03.45."

"Right oh! Cloud cover?"

"Makes no different on a night like this, but Cumulus over Yorkshire at 2500 to 3000 feet skip."

"Roger. What is it tonight? Lincoln isn't it? Big old bird."

"Out of Dalcross, Inverness. I guess they'll be happy to be this far south. They're testing one of those fangled Automatic Gun Laying Turrets."

"Hm. Hope they didn't *load it* by mistake!"

"Yeah, but that's not the only tricky thing tonight. I have to practice my low-altitude radar detection! That means I'm the most important person here. The area will be thick with ground reflections from at least four mountains over 4000 feet. So be careful not to hit anything. You're responsible for getting me home safely!"

"Okay Mister VIP. I will!"

The two men watched their various gauges and did their work, almost without speaking, until Specs announced they were over Kendal in the Lake District, their Initial Point.

"Descend to 5000 feet, no lower. Vector 350, maintain present air speed."

"Do we get to check in with the target?"

"Nope. Strict radio silence."

"Boy, that's tough. Let's hope they're here."

"They've been told to stooge around until we, I, find them."

The engine note changed slightly as Sam compensated for the increased airspeed during the descent.

"5000 feet," Sam announced. "Levelling off. Now what? Can't see anything out there."

"They'll be on your starboard bow, flying vector 320, or thereabouts. You should see a white, flashing light under their tail. But try to ignore it until the last moment. Us intellectual types have to practise."

"Okay. Do your stuff!"

"I have 'em! They're on the scope. Wait a minute. Something seems wrong. Somebody's buggering around with us!"

"What's wrong?"

"They're ten miles ahead skip – correct bearing, but nearly 2000 feet too low."

Sam's mind raced while he pondered what to do. Finally, he said:

"Well, it's our last trip. The Meteors are already parked at base. I don't want to mess this up. Do you?"

"No."

"It must be special instructions, designed to really test you. That's what the RAF is like mate. They throw in these things to keep you on your toes. Let's go down. Just tell me about those ground reflections, because I don't think I would see a mountain out there, if I could *touch it*!"

"Right skip. They'll do one-eighty in about one minute, so let's keep on this heading for a minute and then I'll bring you down behind them, going east."

"Roger that."

Specs swivelled his seat back to review his navigation maps and calculate a course:

"Okay. Make a gentle left turn to vector 220 and descend to 3000. We daren't go lower than that. Think you can get a bead on them?"

"I reckon so. I agree with you, that's low enough. Turning now."

The Mosquito banked in the black night over Scafell Pike before straightening out in a gentle dive.

"I thought I saw something; a light, level with the wing tip," Sam called out.

"Blinking?"

"No."

"Shit."

"Lower?"

"No. I don't think so. Target half mile ahead, bearing ninety degrees exactly. At least they can navigate. Vector 10 now and aim that gun camera."

The Mosquito had been fitted with a bright stroboscopic light instead of a gun. Even on the blackest night, if the target came within their sights when Sam pressed the trigger, the camera would capture an image of the target for confirmation of the 'kill.'

"Armed and ready," Sam said.

"Closing, closing. 2000 feet, 1500 ... 1000! Now! Fire!"

But the mountains around them suddenly lit up, as if a flash gun had gone off. A bright explosion of white and red in front of them erupted where the Avro Lincoln had been and Sam saw burning balls of fire tumbling across gorse and rocks on a mountain's lip.

"Bloody hell!" he yelled. "They hit!"

Sam could see a crag, just below the lip of the mountain, and he had only a fraction of a second to react. He yanked back on the Mosquito's stick and the nose lifted momentarily, but then they entered the debris field of the exploding Lincoln and something hit the port engine. Its propeller sheared off and the left wing dipped. Sam felt the bottom of the aircraft hit something solid. The resulting jolt almost made him bite off his tongue and he couldn't see for the exploding bits of aircraft, but instinct told him to push the right throttle lever fully forward and apply full boost. Slowly, slowly, the port wing came up and the aircraft seemed to stabilise.

"Put your landing lights on!" Specs yelled.

"Good idea."

In the glare of the powerful lights they could see they were slowly losing height, but they had cleared the mountain.

"How the hell did you do *that*?" Specs shouted. "I saw the mountain! I thought we'd bought it for sure! You bloody miracle."

"We're not home yet. Not by a long way. I don't know how long we can stay up like this. Something hit the aircraft, underneath!"

"Yeah! The mountain! I can see a bloody great hole where the bomb bay was."

"Oh. We're losing oil pressure fast. And she's very heavy on the stick. Can you help me?"

"What do I do?"

"See that lever there? It dumps all the fuel in the port tanks. We don't need all that weight now. Pull it."

"Right."

The starboard engine screamed at full power while the engine casings began to glow white-hot.

"Okay. Find the nearest aerodrome. We can't get far like this. The drag from damage is making this as aerodynamic as a brick."

"Right. Hold on. Okay I have them. Can you turn?"

"Not a good idea. Lose too much height."

"Okay. Has to be Cark. It's about Vector 090 from here. Do what you can. I'll get onto them." Sam heard Specs call up Cark: "May Day. May Day. This is Mosquito, Interceptor 241, out of Finningley. We're about 20 miles east of Scafell Pike, descending on one engine. Losing oil pressure rapidly. Request immediate permission to land and fire services. Over."

The radio emitted only static for a few moments before they heard the weak reply:

"Interceptor 241. This is Cark. You have permission to land. Do you have wounded on board? Over."

"Negative. But we are below 2000 feet. We will have to fly down the valleys. Will do our best to reach you. Over."

"Roger. Keep us informed. Good luck. Standing by."

"Can you see anything Sam?"

"Bloody little. Without these lights, we would be up the Khyber Pass. I'm turning into a valley to our right. We just crossed a village with a large church. Any ideas?"

"No. Let me see if Cark can pick us up."

"Cark, this is Interceptor 241. We are flying blind. Can you see us? Over?"

"Negative 241. Give us a landmark, so we can help you."

"Come up here Specs," Sam yelled, as the remaining engine began to misfire badly. "See if you can see anything! If this valley is a dead end, we're stuffed."

They both peered into the blackness. An occasional light flickered past them, but they could see nothing distinctive.

"Up ahead skip. See it?"

"I see it. But I can't see a way through."

In front of them an escarpment led up to a jagged edge slightly above them that cut off their escape route.

"Turn on the navigation lights too. Maybe we can see something to the side."

Sam turned on the lights, which began to flash red on the port wing, green on the starboard. They didn't illuminate very much, but suddenly Specs yelled:

"How about *that*? Portside."

"Looks like we don't have any choice."

A narrow valley branched off from the one they were following, so Sam banked the Mosquito and aimed for the gap. The ground rose until it almost touched the tips of the aircraft's one remaining propeller blade, but they skimmed over a high saddle and dropped into another valley.

"There's a river underneath!" Specs yelled.

"If we follow it, we might be okay."

After a few minutes, they could just make out the reflection of starlight between clouds on an unusually shaped patch of water.

"Cark," Specs said into his radio microphone. "We just passed over a double lake. Small with two wide bits of water joined by a thin bit. Like a dumbbell. Over."

"Give us a minute."

"What do they say?" Sam asked.

"Wait."

They both waited tensely.

"Cark here. It has to be Elter Water. Are you going East still?"

"Roger that."

"Good. Follow the river to Windermere. At least you can ditch there if you have lost too much height. Over."

"They're saying we're not far from Windermere, if we follow the river. We can ditch there skip."

"Are they crazy? With a bloody great hole in the bomb bay. Tell them ditching is not an option."

"Cark. Ditching not an option. We should be okay now. I will check my maps. Over."

"Roger Interceptor 241."

"Well? How much further?" Sam asked.

"Wait a moment."

Specs rummaged furiously through his maps and found Windermere.

"I see a large expanse of water coming up!" Sam yelled. "I can't keep this girl up much longer. 500 feet!"

"We can make it skip! Follow the lake to the end and the river out of it. Cark is about 5 miles from the mouth, on the right. I will get them to light up."

"Cark, turn on every light you have. We're coming in along the river. What bearing for the easiest runway? Over."

"One hundred ten degrees. Repeat, one hundred and ten degrees. What is your altitude? Over."

"Altitude skip?"

"350!"

"Cark we are 350 feet. Over."

"Right. Turn right before you see the railway bridge across the estuary. We are at 60 feet above sea level. Repeat 60 feet. But there are two hills of about 150 feet altitude on the headland shore. The railway runs just south of the southern one. You need to aim between them. Over."

"Roger."

"We need to turn to one hundred and ten degrees just before we see the railway bridge skip. Then steer between two hills, each about 150 feet. Cark is at 60 feet. We should make it."

"If you say so. 300 feet. Well, there's the estuary."

"The map says the bridge is a bit further. About three miles."

The starboard engine coughed three more times and began to belch smoke, of which they were only aware, because it obscured the winking green navigation light.

Both men held their breaths. The engine stopped coughing and continued to roar, but with an uneven beat.

"She's about to seize," Sam said.

Specs pulled out his St. Christopher medallion and kissed it.

"Where's that damned bridge?" Sam yelled. "I don't see it!"

"It must be there. See it? A red signal."

"I hope you're right. Turning now. This is going to kill our height."

But they had come too close to the most southerly hill. Sam had to turn tighter than he would have liked and by the time they were on a heading of 110 degrees, they were at only 140 feet.

"There are the lights!" Specs called, slapping Sam on the shoulder. "Bloody marvellous!"

"I see them. Gear down."

They both felt the two jolts as both wheels locked down.

"Thank God!" Sam declared.

The engine kept running while their wheels touched the grass, just short of the runway, coughed one last time and died. They rolled to a gentle stop at the far end of the runway, exhausted but alive.

* * *

The airfield's crash tenders and fire engines blared in the night, waking all the locals, as emergency crews swarmed toward the crippled Mosquito. A jet of foam sprayed over the still white-hot engine, but it did little more than tick until it cooled, first to a sullen red and then back to blackened metal, the paint having long burned away.

An investigation later proved that the Avro Lincoln, which had flown from RAF Scampton to Dalcross, had then taken off without its altimeter having been recalibrated. Furthermore, the altimeter light had broken and since pre-flight checks had taken place with cockpit lighting off for night flights, the pilot hadn't seen the problem. Scampton is at 36 feet altitude, while

Dalcross is at 1925 feet. Thus, the pilot had believed their height to be almost 2000 feet higher than it really had been.

The RAF praised Sam for his skill in bringing his aircraft home. He began converting to the Gloster Meteor the next day.

Chapter Six

A state of uneasy truce had existed between North Korea, supported by China and Russia, and South Korea, supported by the United Nations, since 1945. On 25th June, 1950 North Korean forces crossed the truce line and invaded South Korea. On 27th June the UN nations adopted S/RES/83 and 21 countries began the defence of South Korea.

Although the United Kingdom sent ground and sea forces, they did not send frontline RAF squadrons. Instead, a few RAF pilots volunteered to serve with the Royal Australian Air Force, which sent squadrons into battle.

Sam flew Gloster Meteors for 616 Squadron until 21st July, 1951, gaining a great deal of respect from fellow pilots and the Squadron Leader. On 7th July, he had seen a notice on the mess wall, announcing that pilots could volunteer to exchange with Australian pilots if they wished to gain combat experience in Korea. The general feeling among RAF pilots was that the Chinese and Russians could not have any aircraft as good as our own, so Sam volunteered. Two weeks later he received a letter notifying him that his application had been successful and that he had been assigned to 77 Squadron, flying Gloster Meteors. He hadn't expected to succeed and now had to tell Brigitte. He handed the letter across the kitchen table and watched her face.

"Sam, this is ridiculous! You can't go! Please tell me; *why* did you volunteer?"

"It's too late. I didn't expect to be accepted."

"Oh, you men! But you don't *have* to go! It's a *war*! People get *killed*! But why did you volunteer in the first place?"

"Because it might be the only way I get practical frontline experience. It will speed up promotion, if nothing else."

This sop did little to assuage Brigitte's fears. She lowered the hand holding the letter to the table and pressed her other palm against her hot brow.

"You know you're just like your brother?" she murmured.

Sam knew this tone of voice and realised that he was in for a sharp lesson.

"You both believe you can walk on water." she continued, still in a murmur. "Well, look where it has got *him*! And I don't think you have *his* luck. If you go to Korea, don't expect to find Jake and I still waiting. I already lost my family in Germany. I have no intention of waiting around to be a weeping widow!"

Until he left for Korea, Sam and Brigitte spoke only in monosyllables. He had no doubt about her intentions, but he had made a commitment.

Arriving at Kimpo airbase, near Seoul, on 24th July, Sam immediately began familiarising himself with the Gloster Meteor F.8 and the USAAF's way of doing things. The United States Air Force controlled the airbase, so Sam encountered a very cosmopolitan crowd there; friendly and serious, determined to get things done and end the War quickly.

Sam's commanding officer assigned Flight Lieutenant Eddie Tucker to be his buddy and showed him to Tucker's hut on the edge of the field. The irony of the Aussie's first name wasn't lost on Sam, but he quickly became friends with the athletic man, who had film star black hair and blue eyes.

"So what's it like up there?" Sam asked as soon as his head hit the camp-bed. "Must be fine. I guess the anti-aircraft stuff is pretty rough?"

"It is," Tucker replied, "but not as tough as the MiGs. We have had a few close shaves already. Thank god nobody's bought it yet."

"Oh, they can't really be *that* bad."

Tucker didn't answer.

Sam had his introduction to the MiG phenomenon during his first sortie on 29th August. He and the other pilots in action that day rose early, ate their bacon and eggs and sauntered over to the Operations tent for the briefing. A few of the older pilots looked pale, but the younger ones, including the three newly arrived British pilots, looked eager for action.

"Now, for the benefit of our visitors, let me explain the situation here," Group Captain Ron Hurst began. Sam saw the deep respect the men had for Hurst by their silent attention. Hurst tapped the map of North Korea's border with a stick and continued, "The Yalu River marks the boundary between North Korea and China. Now the enemy jets, MiG-15s or 'Faggots' as the Yanks have codenamed them, come across the river to strike and fly back over it to get away. We're forbidden to cross that river. And I mean *forbidden*. Any pilot here who breaks *that* rule will not only be court-martialled, but probably worse. So, don't break *that* rule. But it does put us in a difficult position and these pilots are *good*! Make no mistake, *we* are at the disadvantage here. Even the Yanks' F-86 Sabre is no match for the MiG-15s, and they're the best we've got! That's from the horse's mouth and you can quote me. It's also why we call this whole area MiG Alley." Hurst swept the stick across the whole border with China. "They own the border area. That's why we're sticking to ground attack. Stay away from those MiGs. Get in, get out and keep close to the ground whenever you can. And if you do get bounced, stick together. That's the best chance you've got. I will be leading the group, so let's get down to the nitty-gritty, as you poms say."

A nervous chuckle went around the room, but Sam could see the pep-talk had sobered them all up. Nevertheless, when they took off he still felt confident.

Sam formed up as wingman to Tucker and they roared off at 33,000 feet, toward the target near the Chinese border. They were following Hurst's section of three. Sam's Meteor carried two 1000 lb bombs, but Tucker and his other wingman carried sixteen 3-inch rockets. All the Meteors had four 20mm cannons.

Both sections had a different target around a village, which had become notorious as a North Korean stronghold. Sam's target would be a bridge, but intelligence had been sketchy on how well-defended it would be. Fifty miles out from the target, they descended to 5000 feet in a long sweeping dive. This gave them greater speed as they neared MiG Alley. Five miles out from the Initial Point, they dropped to 1000 feet.

"Stick close to the ground Sam," Tucker said. "Dewey and I will be slightly ahead and cover you. Only use your cannons if you see something tasty. You'll need them later. This should be a piece of cake."

"Roger Eddie."

Sam almost laughed hysterically at how bawdy his reply sounded and then understood that he already felt slightly jumpy.

The mixture of rough vegetation, farm tracks and paddy fields shot by his windscreen like a speeded-up movie. He had little time to see anything specific, but when he glanced out of the side of his canopy, he caught a glimpse of a girl in a blue smock and white straw hat, staring at him. He tried to think of her as the enemy, but the thought made him feel queasy.

'I'm going to bomb her friends, maybe even her mum and dad!' he thought. 'Jesus!'

Suddenly Sam wanted to be at home in Finningley. He caught a glimpse of Brigitte in his head, but had to push it away.

"Need to concentrate," he told himself.

As the target came closer his senses and reactions became pin sharp. He felt one with the Meteor, which had proved easy to fly and made him feel safe. The twin-engine jet fighter bucked and weaved through valleys and over low hills, complying with his slightest whim.

"There's the bridge Sam. Take your time," Tucker told him.

Sam armed his bombs and released the safety catch on the bomb release. He wriggled to settle further into his seat, but almost jerked the stick sideways when both Tucker and Dewey opened fire on some trucks either side of the gorge.

All hell broke loose. From both ends of the bridge and numerous positions around the valley, a vicious hail of anti-aircraft fire arced toward him and the others. Sam saw a strike on his right wing and had to bite his lip to ignore it. He had the bridge in his sights. Half a second later he dropped his bombs.

The Meteor bucked upward, so Sam caught the motion with a forward dab on the stick and banked to turn right where the valley forked and follow Tucker.

"One hit Sam," came the level voice of Dewey, who had assigned himself the role of observer.

"Let's get out of here," Tucker added. "Begin ascent to 10,000 at the end of this valley. If you see anything you like, take a few shots Sam, but only a few."

"I'll save 'em."

"Oh! These poms are not so Gung-Ho! as we've been led to believe!" Dewey commented.

They began their climb. Far to their right they saw Hurst's section.

Sam's section had almost reached 10,000 feet when a pilot from the other section pressed his radio microphone button and announced:

"Bandits, 17,000 or more, coming down fast. MiGs! At least 20!"

Hurst came over the radio:

"Break! Break! Turn into them and climb!"

"Follow me Sam!" Tucker added.

Sam followed Eddie Tucker into a climbing bank to the right, but he had barely squared up on the approaching dots when one of them opened fire on him. Three lines of cannon shells shot across the top of his canopy and hit his tail, making the Meteor judder. Sam held on to the stick and continued to climb. He heard a calm voice in his ear:

"I'm hit. Going down."

"Bail Dewey," Tucker replied.

"Affirmative."

Sam tried to see behind him. He could see a white trail of smoke from something and guessed it to be Dewey's stricken Meteor, but the trail vanished below his wing as he kept climbing.

"Stick to me Sam," Tucker said. "We'll be fine. I think I see Dewey's chute."

But it would not be that easy to escape the MiGs, which had turned in pursuit. Sam could not believe their rate of climb, far in excess of the Meteors'.

"Bank to the left and follow me over the MiGs," Tucker told him. "We'll run for home."

Sam did as instructed and saw the MiG's turning onto their tails, but Tucker had levelled out now and led him in a shallow dive toward their own lines. The MiGs levelled out too, guessing Tucker's game, and gave pursuit, but thought better of it when friendly fire covered Tucker and Sam. Even so, the MiGs had only been a few miles behind at the time.

When they landed, they found Hurst's section already home, all aircraft damaged and with one Meteor's fuselage so riddled with cannon holes that the aircraft would have to be scrapped.

Sam didn't sleep that night.

***

On a freezing Friday afternoon in December, 1950, Hooker called all the Rolls Royce project managers into his office at Derby. He had pushed his desk into a corner and propped a large blackboard up on it. This looked like something unprecedented to the men standing there. He cleared his throat and began:

"Gentlemen. We have a problem. Reports are leaking out about the new Russian MiG-15, code name 'Faggot.' The latest information is that its rate of climb is at least better than anything we have, by a long way. Estimates vary up to 10,000 feet per minute."

Hooker waited for the intakes of breath and whistles to finish before continuing:

"Now I needn't point out that the Meteor, using the Derwent engine of course, has a rate of climb of 7000 feet per minute. That means we have to roll out the new Avon *much* faster, but the Government also expects unrest in the Far East and wants an upgrade to the Meteor right away. So, what do we have?"

Men began to stick up their arms and make suggestions, principally modifications to the Nene, but Edward couldn't hear them. If he had spoken or looked at anyone during the rest of the meeting, they would have heard only platitudes, or seen a blank expression. He could not believe what had happened.

'The Russians have upgraded the Nene somehow,' he thought. 'But how's that possible?'

His day grew worse at the end of the meeting when Hooker held him back and Sanderson arrived.

"We need a quick chat Edward," Hooker said.

Edward nodded.

"Questions are being asked at a very high level. How did the Russians get such a powerful engine so quickly? Have they modified the Nene? Is there anything you can tell us that might help us fill in the gaps?"

"No," Edward replied. "I know absolutely no way they could have the information about alloys for the rotors to be able to turn at the speeds required. Unless they have built a completely new engine."

Hooker and Sanderson looked at each other.

"Well," said Sanderson. His voice sounded full of restrained self-importance. "It's my job to find out what happened, so I have set up an internal investigation and I'm putting Baker in charge."

Edward's heart sank. The older and senior Baker had been the team leader for the Derwent programme during WWII and his biggest rival, so Edward knew this could not go well.

"One last thing Edward. I am sorry to say that M.I.6 want to speak to you about this today. They're waiting outside. Are you ready?"

"Yes. I suppose so."

Hooker and Sanderson shuffled out and two men entered, one of them looking remarkably like The Vapour, without a hat and coat. When he lit up one of those familiar cigarettes, Edward could no longer be in doubt.

"Hello Edward. Sorry we have to meet again."

"Oh. Hello."

"I have some bad news."

"Oh?"

"I will get straight to the point. The Soviet Union appears to not only have modified your Nene engine, but to have copied and improved it. That can only mean one thing."

"What?" Edward knew the truth but, he didn't want to believe, or say, it.

"They somehow got hold of the alloys they needed. We need to know how."

"I ... I can't help you."

The Vapour stood up and paced the room slowly, thinking.

"The point is; I can't help *you* unless you give us something. We know your brother, Sam, is a pilot in the RAF. Suppose he had to face a Russian pilot with a superior engine? An engine that used parts... or ideas... stolen from us? Give us *something*. It will go easy for you, if you... made a mistake and you tell us now."

"Hm! I told you what I tried to do to protect us. As far as I can tell, they got away with *nothing*. I gave *you* the original shavings."

"Yes, and Rolls Royce has analysed them and two of them are virtually identical, no good to the Russians. The third is not much different. In other words, as I understand it, there would not have been enough information for the Russians to engineer the secret alloy themselves."

"No, that can't be right. At least I don't believe so ... ."

The Vapour took a metal tin from his pocket and opened it. He placed the lid on Hooker's desk and folded back two pieces of white cloth to display the tin's contents.

Edward immediately knew something had gone wrong. He expected to see two fairly straight shavings and one with a distinctive curl, but all three were almost straight. His heart thumped in his chest.

"I ... I don't know. They look similar, but one looks wrong."

"Really? How?" The Vapour's voice sounded dismissive, almost sarcastic.

"One should have a tight curl at its end. Have you changed them?"

"No Edward."

"I don't know. I'm not lying. These don't look like the ones I gave you."

"Well, could they have been swapped?"

"No! No! It's just not possible. No. They were in my jacket the whole time ... after I had to take them out of my desk, in my office. I presume it was your chaps who went through my desk. But I couldn't risk leaving them there. It forced me to take them out. Unless your chaps swapped them?"

"The Vapour perched on the edge of Hooker's desk and rubbed his forehead:"

"I see. This is just one big mess."

The Vapour looked at the other man, shorter, more serious. Edward assumed him to be his usual interrogator's superior. The man's expression revealed no emotion.

"Alright," The Vapour concluded. "You can go, but I will want to speak to you in a week or so; you might remember something."

Both men turned and left, closing the door softly behind them. Edward stared into space, but after five minutes had passed, nobody had come, so he went back to his office.

Rolls Royce moved him to a nominal position, overseeing engine tests. This meant that he would have no direct control over any technical teams, or access to information about secret alloys, or any other secret materials.

'This is it. They no longer trust me,' he thought. 'In a company like Rolls, it's the beginning of the end.'

The Vapour visited every few weeks, but Edward didn't tell him what he had already worked out. He had sat, staring into space in his Derby flat, hour after hour, trying to work out how the Russians did it. This is the train of thought that preoccupied him:

It seemed obvious that the Russians had swapped the shavings. They could have only have taken them while he and Yulia were sleeping in her Suite on the Thursday night, but how could they have known the shavings were in his jacket, surely the most unlikely hiding place?

Finally, he cracked the problem:

"Yes! Yes! That's it. I remember mentioning that they were in my jacket to Yulia. But why did she tell them? No, they must have had her bedroom bugged! So obvious! What a fool! She was the bait all along and I fell for it! Then they swapped the shavings. Yes! But how? Didn't she lock the room? I saw her lock it! Or did she?"

These thoughts came to Edward at 3 am, in March, 1951. The black of night is never a good time to reason and his fears about Yulia flooded back into his mind, like the water from a breaking dam. Yet those waters were quickly channelled into a single thought:

"Yulia must have tricked me!"

Only the walls heard him, but his grief for a love lost began to seep into those walls, so that he no longer felt life worth living. He moved his bed to a room that let in more light, a room where he could watch the sky, but he saw no good omens.

He heard nothing more about MiG-15s, except what he could catch in newspaper reports about the new war in Korea. His original teams avoided him and Sanderson only seemed to gloat over his demise. There were no more offers to play golf and Baker seemed especially smug. Edward was finished. But he still hoped that Sam would be safe, because the newspapers had announced that the RAF wouldn't participate in the War.

It came as a supreme shock therefore when Sam rang him early one evening in July to announce his transfer to Korea.

"But you *can't* go Sam!" he yelled down the telephone.

"But I *am*! What's wrong old chap? You never shout like that?"

"Sam. Listen to me. This is a war. The Russians are great pilots and they have a good aircraft in the MiG-15. You mustn't go!"

"Sorry Eddie, but I'm leaving tomorrow."

"No Sam! No!"

"Hey! Don't worry! I'll be fine. Chin up old man! You don't want dad to hear you talking like this."

Edward's eyes filled with tears when Sam said:

"Sorry. I have to go. I'll write, regularly. Keep an eye on Brigitte for me. In fact, that's one reason I called. We argued. She doesn't want me to go and says she'll leave. If she does, please keep a special eye on Jake. For *me*?"

"Sam?"

"Eddie?"

"Yes. Of course. But if there's any way to get out of it or get home early, take it. Don't ask questions. Just do what I say, for *me*?"

"Oh. You ask a lot. I'll try Eddie. Cheerio!"

Edward slumped into his sofa and didn't move until the flat had fallen into darkness.

The next few months spent waiting for news from Sam would be an agony of torture for him.

***

On 22nd September, Sam flew on another mission, led by Flight Commander Hurst, to destroy another North Korean stronghold.

The Flight Commander, a WWII veteran, had the trust and confidence of every man in the Flight and had become not only a leader, but an icon, to them.

The Flight attacked a village with rockets under very heavy and accurate anti-aircraft fire. Most of the aircraft sustained damage, including Sam's. But Tucker's Meteor lost one engine and had little aileron control left. As he struggled to gain height, both Tucker's wingmen tried to protect him.

"MiG's, 11 o'clock high! I count three, four, five … . Breaking!" somebody yelled into the radio. All eyes craned for the silver devils. Sam saw them just in time and jinked to avoid a cannon burst. It passed to the right of his wing and just missed Tucker's aircraft.

"Coming round Tucker! Hang on," Sam radioed.

"Roger that. It's getting hot."

Sam banked hard right and came round behind the MiG, which had begun to turn for a clean shot at Tucker. Sam aimed and tried to get a burst off, but the MiG had seen him and banked away, so he removed his thumb from the trigger.

"Shit! Pursuing."

"No. Leave him!" Tucker's new wingman, Dillon, radioed.

Both Meteors fell in with Tucker's stricken aircraft, Sam above and ahead, Dillon below and behind.

"Look above you Sam!" Dillon called out.

"Damn!" Sam saw another silver bullet coming straight at him from above, so had no choice, but to take evasive action. He pulled the throttles back and activated the air-brakes, slowing the Meteor by 100 knots and almost shaking his teeth loose.

This brought him back behind Tucker's aircraft, giving him a shot at the MiG as it dove in front of him. But it proved too fast and a second MiG came down behind his leader, unseen.

"Watch out! Bank!" Dillon yelled into the radio for both pilots. Sam instinctively yanked the stick to the right, but Tucker knew he couldn't do this. A heavy burst of cannon fire raked his fuselage, from the nose to just behind the wings. The canopy shattered and Sam saw Tucker slump forward, covered in blood, while the Gloster Meteor eased over into a dive.

"Bail out Tucker!" Sam yelled.

But Tucker didn't reply. His Meteor dove straight into a hillside.

The MiGs seem to have found better prey for now, so Sam and Dillon headed for where they had last seen the others. Below them a section of three Meteors fought with two MiGs. Only one of the Australian aircraft flew up to join them when the MiGs seemed to have had enough and headed back toward the Yalu River.

"Identify, red section survivor," another pilot called out.

They heard only heavy breathing in response for a while, before the survivor gasped:

"Arpisella. Jeez! They got Hurst!"

"Let's go home!" the first pilot replied.

But an argument broke out. Some of pilots wanted to chase the last two MiGs, which were still banking to the south east. Sam realised that in 18 sorties he hadn't yet even fired a shot at a MiG. He wanted his chance, so when one of the Meteors turned to follow the retreating MiGs, he followed.

Sam pushed his throttle levers fully forward and put the Meteor into a shallow dive.

"We'll catch them!" radioed the pilot ahead. "Who's following?"

"Torrens!"

"Beerbelly here. Welcome to the ride!"

"You think they're out of ammo?"

"I reckon so, don't you?"

The idea that the MiGs would leave easy targets behind while they still had ammunition seemed preposterous.

"Yeah."

"Watch your six."

Sam turned to look out of rear of his canopy, but they were completely alone with the MiGs in the dome of blue.

Though they had the advantage of height and pushed their jet fighters to the limit, Sam and Beerbelly saw the MiGs gradually recede in their windscreen view. They had no chance of catching the little Soviet jets and finally Beerbelly said:

"Yalu River coming up! I'm low on fuel. Turning for home Torrens. You coming?"

"Give me a few more minutes. You never know."

"No. I gotta go. I'll steer bearing 120 and keep my speed down. Catch me up."

"Roger."

"Good luck, but I reckon the little blighters are already thinking about their bush tucker."

Sam pushed on at full throttle until he knew the silver band of the Yalu River lay directly below him. His frustration got the better of him. He released the safety catch on his gun trigger and pressed the red button. An arc of shells curved forward and down, falling miles short of the vanishing MiGs. He banked sharply and headed after Beerbelly. Half way home he caught him and they both landed together.

"Did you get one?" his ground crew chief asked, seeing that rounds had been fired.

Sam shook his head. News of Hurst's death hadn't gone right around the airfield yet, but as soon as it had, a deathly silence had fallen over the wide strip of land. If anybody spoke at all in the mess it was about Hurst, or something banal. Sam pushed down a glass of scotch in remembrance of Tucker and headed for the empty hut to write the letter that he had put off for so long:

> *Dear Eddie,*
> *I have been writing regularly to Brigitte, but I have not been able to write to you. It is not as easy as I thought.*

There, Sam stopped. He wanted to say that the Squadron had been decimated, but of course it would have been censored. In the end, he decided that the second sentence had to be as good a way as any of telling his brother what he meant.

'Even *that* might get edited!' he thought.

He thought of a code that only Eddie would understand, so that he could give his brother an impression of what had happened. So many pilots had been killed by MiGs that the code word 'log' had become common usage in letters. When he had finished, he felt unhappy with what he had written, but decided to send it anyway.

***

Edward tore open Sam's letter and looked at the blacked-out sections with dismay. It read:

> *Dear Eddie,*
>
> *I have been writing regularly to Brigitte, but I have not been able to write to you. It is not as easy as I thought. Do you remember the log we floated down the river at Silvertops? Brigitte often mentions it. Well, I wish I could sleep like that, like a 'log,' but I don't. The weather is good though and the locals are friendly enough. The other pilots have been great sports, but we don't get much time for anything other than a [blacked out] in the bar.*
>
> *I have flown [blacked out] sorties, most over [blacked-out]. We lost our [blacked out] the other day. I haven't [at least ten words blacked-out]*
>
> *They give us [at least 15 words blacked-out].*
>
> *[A whole paragraph blacked-out]*
>
> *Well, that is all my news. You can write to me at the address overleaf. Give my love to Brigitte if you speak to her, and remember your promise to look after Jake.*
>
> *When you write, tell me how things are going at [blacked out].*
>
> *Sam*

Edward read the letter three times before making himself a cup of tea and sitting down to consider its cryptic message. He knew Sam wanted to tell him something, because he couldn't remember any log in the river at Silvertops. He knew Brigitte certainly wouldn't.

"Log? Log? Log?" he wondered. "Perhaps something about the Meteor? It isn't known as a great aircraft, but it has no major vices that I know of. Perhaps some other aircraft? I hope so, because I know nothing about Korea, if it's anything else!"

Hooker's pep talk came back to him and his use of the word 'Faggot.'

Edward wasn't too familiar with the word and had to check a dictionary, before he felt sure.

"Yes! That *must* be it!"

Edward's heart sank like a stone, seeming to drop into a pool of cold water that had settled in his stomach.

"My own brother is suffering and might be killed because of my own, stupid incompetence!"

His anguished voice echoed around his lounge walls. He felt he could bear it no longer. His life had become a black abyss and there seemed no way out. Yulia didn't love him, Ewa was dead and now his brother might die because of *him*. These thoughts were so black that they scarcely took form. He could only moan and swim through a morass of self-loathing. Each day became a prison of fear while he waited a letter of a different kind.

His thoughts began to return to the long holidays in the Bailiff's lodge on the estate, searching for something, some lost memory. He missed Yulia terribly and imagined a conversation with her about the lodge.

"So this summer – I was twelve, remember – my mum didn't talk much. She sat in the sun, in a beautiful white summer dress and looked up at the sun. But I couldn't see her eyes, because she wore sunglasses all the time. I had the feeling she wanted to be alone, so I kept away. But I finally asked my father what was wrong. He said, 'Son, there's no such thing as the perfect woman; they either love you too much or not at all!' He avoided me after that and I guess he was glad we had Brigitte.

"Who was she?"

"I told you. She was our nanny – I guess you would call her an au pair nowadays – from Germany. My father had to hire her for the summer to take care of us."

"Oh yes. Freckles."

"Yes. I was always an introvert, always had my head in books too, but I wasn't what you would call a *thinker*. I was happy to see *others* happy and I just enjoyed being part of a crowd. I liked just *going along for the ride*. Do you know what I mean?"

"Yes."

"But I never forgot what my father said. Actually, I think it's the only time he ever spoke to me about women. But I don't think that's why it stuck in my head.

"Sam and I – sometimes Suzy – would spend all day playing in the woods, or swimming in the pool. We had a wood near our house in Dorking too and I always loved being there. I felt like a king.

"But each wood is different. They talk to you. I remember spending hours, lying on my back in fern brakes, trying to feel the ... spirit of the wood near the big house. It felt older, and darker, than the wood at Dorking. I liked it and talked to it ... ."

"Talked to the wood? Ha! Ha!"

"Oh, you're laughing at me. It must sound silly ... ."

"Funny, not silly."

"It was the trees actually. I talked to this big oak tree. It seemed to have a face, and once I thought it answered me, but it was only a crow with a speech defect!"

"Ha! You are so *funny*! What does this mean?"

"It warbled rather than 'cawed.' Anyway, I taught Sam to swim and he taught Susan to swim while I talked with Brigitte. You see, she wouldn't stop engaging me in conversation about politics. I guess it was because I wasn't that much younger than her and my father ignored her.

"Every evening we would take tea. Brigitte would go out with my father during the morning and buy some provisions at a nearby town; bread, jam, ham, that sort of thing, although Brigitte avoided eating the ham, and I didn't know it then, but mum had to cook it. But at about 9 pm, just as the fireflies appeared and the golden light went out, the butler would bring a tray of ginger beer and goodies from the main house; ginger-snaps, chocolate cake, biscuits … . Things like that. So, Sam and I often avoided tea in the hope of stuffing ourselves at supper time. But we did eat tea this particular day and Brigitte turned her freckled face to me and said, 'I don't believe in socialism,' or something like that.

"Mum had gone to bed and my father's face was buried in a paper. Nobody else had raised the subject of politics, so I just stared at her. But then my father lowered the paper and stared at *me*!

"I had never heard my father say anything political and I had few ideas on the subject myself, but I knew his look meant that I should say something. Sam and Susan both waited for my answer. 'Why not?' I asked. 'I thought all Germans supported Socialism. My teacher says it's better than Bolshevism.'

"After this she wouldn't leave me alone on politics. I felt hurt. It felt as if my father had instructed her to debate me on it, but when I tried to draw him in, he avoided the subject. But I think I felt more hurt, because I had been ambushed into making a judgement.

Or at least it sounded like I did. I never like to judge anybody.

"The summer days stretched like an endless golden chain towards a forgotten horizon. Sam and I climbed the trees and I crossed the Impossible River, as we called it, by the branches of a tree. My elation lasted days … .

"My favourite time was early morning. I used to get up earlier than anyone else. There would always be hardboiled eggs, honey and bread in the pantry and I was old enough to make my own breakfast. Then I would go for a long walk by the river. I tried be as quiet as a hunter, but the crows would rise like pall bearers and fly away when they spotted me. I often lay in the navel of dead bracken and stared up at passing clouds … ."

"It sounds so beautiful," she mumbled. "You sound like a poet."

"A very bad one. Anyway, I forgot my anger at father and Brigitte when I was in the woods. But I noticed that, although Sam seemed just as loyal to me, there seemed a question in the air whenever our eyes met. I spent more and more time on my own. I began to learn to think, and understand that I liked it. That's when my thoughts turned again and again to what my father had said about women.

"I suddenly knew that the word 'they' to be the significant one. As I said, I hate judging people, and I never, ever dreamed that my parents were anything less than perfect. But suddenly I saw my father in a cold light. 'They' could only mean that he had been out with more than one woman. But my mother had always said she was his *first* romance. Now I wondered if *he* had caused my mother's illness by having an affair with another woman. I guess that was the end of my innocence. But it was also the birth of a new freedom. I felt as if my thoughts were soaring like an eagle, far above the small, secluded life of Sam and Susan.

"I still pretended to be angry with Brigitte, but actually I wasn't."

"What happened next?"

"I thought you were almost asleep."

Edward would often fall asleep during these long dialogues in his head and wake up, cold and uncomfortable, on the floor of his lounge in the morning.

***

Yulia had finally posted her letter in February, 1951.

She had no idea how long it would take to reach England by the circuitous route she had planned for it. She didn't even know whether Edward still lived at the same address that he had scrawled on a scrap of paper.

Now she sat smoking a cigarette in the open space, watching her son run on the snow. She felt tired and pensive.

A youth of about fifteen scuffed along the path and saw her slim, crossed legs, stretching out from her heavy fur coat. He couldn't see any more of the woman except a few tufts of blonde hair wafting on the frigid air from her hood, but he liked what he saw. He pulled a cigarette, which he had picked up, from behind his ear and straightened it before placing it between his lips and asking:

"Hey! Got a light?"

Yulia turned to face the youth. He saw the lines on her face and looked away. Seeing the little boy, he mumbled:

"Doesn't matter."

***

Sam had been promoted to leader of his own section. The sortie on the 24th September would be his last, before a short leave, during which he planned to see the sights in Seoul. He wanted to do anything that would take his mind off flying. Since Hurst's death they had been told to stick strictly to ground attack, but this hadn't helped much, because they were instructed to fly low. In an attempt to counter this, the new Flight Commander had decided to try raids by sections of three aircraft.

Sam didn't know about the Russian deal with Rolls Royce, or about Edward's part in it, but the little MiGs filled him with terror.

Vladimir Klimov had modified the Nene to produce his first prototype engine, the RD-45. From this he had developed the superior VK-1, which powered the MiG-15. It had far more power than the Derwent in the Meteor and could fully exploit the exotic alloy, Nimonic80a, which the Russians had managed to copy. As a result, the MiG-15 had a rate of climb nearly twice that of the early Gloster Meteors.

'God help me!' Sam thought, as he climbed into his cockpit.

His fingers shook slightly as he led his two wingmen up to 10,000 feet and headed north.

"Too much scotch," he told himself.

They headed for a bridge, just north of Jonchon, but five miles out and at only 3000 feet, Sam's left wingman yelled:

"MiGs! Six of 'em! Six o'clock hi- … !"

The wingman never completed his warning. His Meteor exploded, rocking Sam's meteor as he dove for the nearest valley.

"Following you down Sam," came the calm reassurance from his other wingman. But a moment later Sam heard, "I'm hit. Bailing!"

Sam turned to see if his wingman got out, but he only caught a glimpse of an explosion on a hillside. The three MiGs loomed large in his rear canopy frame.

"This is it. Do or die!" he yelled, pushing the nose forward and jinking along the bottom of a narrow river valley. He almost hit a hill when the valley swung right, but had the satisfaction of seeing six streaks of gunfire rake the paddy fields below him.

A left turn came and went, after which the valley became a gorge, so narrow in one place that Sam had to bank right over, in order that the vertical wings could slip through the narrow wedge of air.

The MiG's chose to go over the top, but they were quickly upon him again, two of them emptying their ammunition into his fuselage. The Meteor began to shake violently, but the engines whistled as smoothly as ever.

One of the MiGs broke away, out of ammunition, while the two others still pursued their prey. A second MiG ran out of ammunition and turned for home. Sam could see no more valleys nearby, so decided to try and out turn the remaining MiG. It proved a mistake. The crafty pilot saw the ploy and with full ammunition boxes, fired a long burst.

Sam saw ragged holes appear in his fuselage and wings, but the engines still sounded fine. Moreover, the MiG had overshot him, so Sam switched to bank left and found himself on the tail of a Soviet fighter for the first time. He pulled up his nose and pressed the red trigger button. A stream of explosive shells from his four cannons raked the MiG's wing, but it continued to fly straight and smooth.

Sam climbed after the MiG, but suddenly understood the foolishness of such a move and banked hard to the right. The MiG pilot banked after him. Sam hoped he could run for home, although he felt so disoriented that he didn't know which way that lay anymore. He pushed the throttles fully forward and checked his compass.

"Facing the wrong way, toward the Yalu River! Have to get away!"

The last became his only lucid thought and he repeated it like a mantra. But looking behind him, he saw the MiG grow larger. He knew the pilot would open fire any second. He waited until he heard cannon fire and pulled the nose up, knowing his only chance would be to exhaust the MiG's ammunition. The two Rolls Royce Derwent engines dragged the Meteor higher into the blue heaven, screaming at full power, but the MiGs engine proved too good.

As Sam struggled toward the heavens, the MiG pilot brought him within range again. But short on ammunition, the enemy pilot waited until he had drawn very close, before opening fire. Sam's last sight was of the port engine exploding, engulfing his whole aircraft in a ball of fire. Before he could eject, the rest of his aircraft exploded, killing him instantly.

The MiG pilot had no time to evade the explosion, but when he emerged unscathed from the other side, he performed a barrel role at the top of the MiG's flight ceiling to celebrate his sixth kill.

***

Edward switched out the light in Test Bed 1 Control Room in case anybody should catch him, but most of the Rolls Royce employees had gone home for the night.

The telephone call from a sobbing Brigitte had come as a bolt from the darkest night in hell:

"Sam's ... dead."

"Oh! God! No!"

"I can't ... speak now Eddie. Can you ... tell dad? I don't think I can. Bye."

For a moment Edward felt confused:

'Dad?'

But then he remembered that Brigitte had no parents and called Dominic 'dad.'

He put down the receiver, still emitting that steady drone, and sat down heavily. His worst nightmare had been visited upon him.

But he still held a glimmer of hope in his heart that Sam's death might not have been caused by a MiG-15.

Two weeks later, that hope vanished.

He opened a letter, posted by airmail from Seoul:

Dear Edward,

I knew your son and I know he would have wanted you to know the truth about his death. I can't tell you much, except that he will sleep like a 'log.' Don't try and contact me, because this is risky for me. I am sorry.

"I don't want to live!" Edward moaned. "What has happened to my life?"

He began planning a way out from that moment. The opportunity arose when Baker asked him to stay late later in the week, to clean up after the test of the newly modified Avon engine.

Edward woke up determined to go through with his plan that day. He almost didn't bother with the battered letter on his doormat, but even with his limited German, he could see that it had a return address in

Dresden, which lay in Soviet occupied Germany. When he slowly tore off the edge of the envelope and pulled out the letter, two black and white photographs fell to the doormat.

Yulia almost filled the first photograph, which Edward guessed could have been taken by herself using a timer, because her smile looked uncertain. The poorly lit room revealed a modern refrigerator and tiled wall in the background. Behind her Edward could further make out a door, and through it, a corridor, dim, but brightly lit at its far end. Yulia wore a plain dress and around her neck, a locket.

Edward stared hard at the image. Her face carried more lines that he remembered. He shuffled Yulia's photograph behind the other and stared at the face of a boy of about three with a mop of dark hair and a cheeky grin on his chubby face. The boy had Yulia's eyes, but there seemed something unsettlingly familiar about his face too. He reminded Edward of Sam.

"Funny. Yulia used to remind me of Sam –or something else – whenever she smiled."

He unfolded the letter and read it carefully:

Dear Edward,

I hope this reaches you, because I am not sure you still live at the same address. I no longer work for the same company, but they gave me a nice flat on the edge of Moscow when I retired. I miss you a lot. I am very happy otherwise and have a little job in a local shop as a counter assistant. It does not pay much, but it stops me getting very bored.

My flat has a lovely view and it is not too cold in the winter. It has a double bed and plenty of space for three, but unfortunately my little boy does not have a father here.

I do not know what to say actually, except that I miss you. I hope you did not get into too much trouble for me and I hope that everything is good. Are Sam and Susan well?

I had to ask a friend in Dresden to post this for obvious reasons. She is a very nice lady and would help anyone in need.

That is all I have to say.

Oh! I nearly forgot! Do you remember the locket? Perhaps you cannot see in this photograph, but there are two Angels singing on the lid.

I love you - always.
Yulia xxxxx

Edward felt like dropping the letter and swearing at Yulia's lies, but instinct took over and forced him to stuff the letter and photographs into his breast pocket.

The letter troubled him all day. Yulia had heavily underlined the words 'company' and 'father here.' Edward knew what the first meant, but the second phrase led him to wonder:

"Could *I* be the boy's father?"

This idea felt like another of Yulia's tricks, so he dismissed it. But the mention of the locket with the two Angels troubled him deeply. It had struck a chord deep inside him, a sound which hadn't stop resonating, even as he arrived at the Rolls Royce factory. He could not make any sense of it at all, but the phrase 'two Angels' seemed enormously significant in some obscure way.

The sun had already set and the factory seemed deserted, a fit setting for what Edward had to do. He had already disabled the master door lock, so that when he pressed the ignition button for the jet engine, he had been able to open the door and walk into the roaring test chamber.

"Giving me this job almost seems like Rolls' way of asking me to copy Don. Well, now I'm going to do it!"

As the engine screamed up to 4000 rpm, he deemed the time to be right. He lowered his head and held onto part of the test bed frame. He didn't want to go too early and mess it up. Life with half a head would be worse than death.

Edward could feel the force of engine suction, pulling at him, standing his hair on end and rocking his eyeballs in their sockets. He felt as if the air were being sucked out of his lungs.

Suddenly an image of two Angels flashed into his mind, followed immediately by an image of Silvertops in the snow. The distant memory of Christmas in the big house suddenly emerged from the gloom of Edward's lost memory and he saw clearly a face, a little girl's face.

The chubby little girl had freckles, blonde hair and that same enigmatic smile as Yulia. He remembered pulling a Christmas cracker with her and that his half of the cracker held a silver locket, inscribed with two Angels, singing.

"Screaming Angels!" he had told her. "You may keep it."

"Thank you. But they are singing, not screaming," the girl replied, leaning forward and kissing him. She ran away, giggling.

"Julia!"

Suddenly it all came back to Edward. Yulia *was* Julia. Somehow she had loved him all these years and now she had found him. Edward wanted to live.

His eyes sought desperately for a way out of his own trap. He could hold onto the frame for only a few moments more against the pull of the air-breathing monster. A red cable near his hand supplied current to the spark plugs that ignite the mixture, but by now heat from the compressed air alone would ignite the mixture, so the engine would not need a spark any more.

Edward felt a rising panic, but tried to force it down. He could see the black cable that ran from the master cut-out switch and would stop power to the fuel pumps. This would be his only chance, but it seemed too far to reach. He knew if he lunged for it with one hand, he would get sucked toward the front of the engine and cut to pieces, but he had no choice. He leaped for the black cable, letting go of the frame with one hand. Feeling his finger-tips close around the cable, he tried to rip it out of its socket. Because of the plug's angle to the cable, this proved impossible, but he saw that somebody hadn't entirely finished the wiring. Tape had been wrapped around a splice in the cable, just above his hand. He slid his hand above the splice, yanked hard and saw the two lengths of wire separate. The lower cable end fell against the engine casing, sending out a cascade of sparks. He tried to hang onto the slippery upper cable, but it slipped from his grasp.

The increasing suction-power from the engine ripped Edward's other hand from the frame and slammed him into a support structure, just in front of the engine intake. He stared into the maw of the fire-breathing dragon, recognising his doom. But the fingers of his left hand were close enough to get a few of them around a bar of the structure, so he hung on tightly while groping with the other hand for a hold. When he found it, he clung on as the engine's revs peaked. His legs were pulled from under him, so that he found him suspended in the air horizontally like some crazy trapeze artist, his feet only inches from the intake rotors. But the screaming Angel beside him began to slow down. When he thought he could hold on no longer, the suction decreased enough for his feet to drop to the ground and he fell to his knees, hands covered in blood.

***

Edward stood in the snow, watching the entrance to the block of flats.

His feet were numb, his fingers bright red and his ears stinging from the cold, but the blood his adrenalin pushed through his veins made him feel warm.

Edward had told himself all the way on the train to Dresden that:

"Perhaps   Julia   never   knew   about   the microphone."

The woman at the return address on Yulia's envelope helped smuggle him across the border into Czechoslovakia, and from there he reached Moscow without difficulty. The hardest part had been slipping out of England unnoticed.

Suddenly the doors swung open and a woman in a fur coat walked through the flurry of snow that whipped around the door. A gust of wind tore a blonde curl of her hair from under her hat and Edward knew it to be Julia.

She walked toward him, sometimes looking at the ground, sometimes grinning. Edward grinned back.

She turned round and shouted, "Come on Edward. Don't be shy!"

The little boy with the brown mop of hair followed her out though the door, ran up to his mother and held her hand. They continued walking until Edward swept Julia into his arms. A tear rolled down his cheek as he said her name for the first time:

"Julia!"

"I thought you wouldn't come."

"So clever of you to contact me via Dresden. But how the hell have you managed all this? I can't work it out!"

"I was there when you crossed the river in the trees. That was the first time I saw you. But you didn't see me. Then there was the Christmas party. You told me you wanted to be an engineer when you grew up. Do you remember the party yet?"

"Yes. I had forgotten until it was almost too late. I'm sorry."

"Don't be. I must have seemed like only a silly little girl then. Anyway, my father owned the big house. His name was Anton Watman. Yes, the English sounding name might be partly why he got his diplomatic post in London. But he also became rich with a business importing vodka. Then somebody in Russia found out and he lost his post. We lost the house too and had to go back to Russia. Shortly after, he disappeared. My mother and I never heard from him again.

"She couldn't afford to feed me, so I went to live with her brother, my uncle Makar. He didn't want me ... then, when I was very young, but *his* brother, Andrei took me in."

"And you never knew about the microphone in your bedroom? That must be how they knew they should swap the shavings?"

"Yes. I didn't know at the time. Sorry. I heard about Sam too. I'm so sorry."

"When I heard about Sam's death and thought you had helped them, I nearly ended it."

"But you did your best!"

"Yes. I know that now."

They began walking back to the door. Edward suddenly asked:

"But how did you engineer our meeting?"

"Your father knew mine through the drinks trade and both knew Hooker. Your dad helped get you the job at Rolls Royce and more recently, persuaded Kirill to employ me and bring me to London when he knew the Russians wanted the Nene engine. Simple really!"

"Yes!"

They both laughed. Julia threw back her head as she did, letting her mouth catch the falling flakes on her teeth.

They hugged each other tightly. Through the ice crystal beneath a low cloud, a crow wheeled down until it could settle upon the lip of the building.

"Edward!" Julia called out. "Come and meet your daddy!"

Author's Note

Edward, Yulia, their families and friends are all fictional, but most of the events in this book actually happened.

The MiG-15 far out-performed allied fighters at the beginning of the Korean War, infuriating the USA, who knew about the strange gift of Nene engines that the British Government had provided. Many allied pilots died as a result of this gift and it wasn't until American designers up-rated the North American F-86 Sabre that the allies finally had an aircraft that could outperform the MiG-15.

Details of Rolls Royce operations at the time are as authentic as I can make them, including locations, equipment and the secret Nimonic alloys used to produce the special engine rotors. The Russians stole the Nimonic80a filings on the soles of specially modified shoes, according to many sources.

Stanley Hooker was a real person, but all other British characters are fictional. All Soviet characters other than Yulia, her family and her friends are real.

Accounts of the British gift are hard to come by and I could only glean information from second-hand accounts by friends of Rolls Royce employees at the time and various Wikipedia articles, including one about the Klimov VK-1 engine.

To my knowledge, this is the first time the extraordinary event has been recorded in a published work.

L.F.
22/05/2017

Biography of Lazlo Ferran

During Lazlo Ferran's extraordinary life, he has been an aeronautical engineering student, dispatch rider, graphic designer full-time busker, guitarist and singer (recording two albums, one of Arabic music featuring the rhythms of Hossam Ramzy). He has traveled widely and had a long and successful career within the science industry, but now left employment in the public sector to concentrate on writing. He has lived and worked in London since 1985 and grew up in the home counties of England.

Brought up as a Buddhist, in recent years he has moved towards an informal Christian belief and has had close contact with Islam and Hinduism. He has a deep and lasting interest in theology and philosophy. His ideas and observations form the core of his novels. Here, evil, good, luck and faith battle for control of the souls who inhabit his worlds.

He has traveled widely, living for a while in Cairo during 1982. Later, he spent some time in Central Asia having various adventures, one of which was getting married in the traditional Kyrgyz style. He has a keen interest in the Far East, Middle East, Asia and Eastern Europe - the latter informing his series of books about vampires and werewolves. He keeps very busy writing in his spare time and pursuing his other interests of history, genealogy and history of the movies.

From the author:

Thank you for reading my story and I hope you liked it. I value very much feedback from people and need this if each book is to be better than the last, so if you could take the time to either post a comment on my blog or simply email me, I would appreciate it.

Where to find Lazlo Ferran
Blog: http://www.lazloferran.com
Email: lazloferran@gmail.com
Lazlo Friend Newsletter: http://eepurl.com/K9r8P

Made in the USA
Columbia, SC
01 December 2017